Pauline Bradford Hopkins

Ye Lyttle Salem Maide

A story of witchcraft

Pauline Bradford Hopkins

Ye Lyttle Salem Maide
A story of witchcraft

ISBN/EAN: 9783744747684

Printed in Europe, USA, Canada, Australia, Japan

Cover: Foto ©Andreas Hilbeck / pixelio.de

More available books at **www.hansebooks.com**

Ye Lyttle Salem Maide

"There keep ye at that distance.
I know your sly ways"

page 75

A Story of Witchcraft

By

Pauline Bradford Mackie

Author of
"Mademoiselle De Berny : A Story of Valley Forge"

Illustrated by

"'This world is very evil,
The times are waxing late"

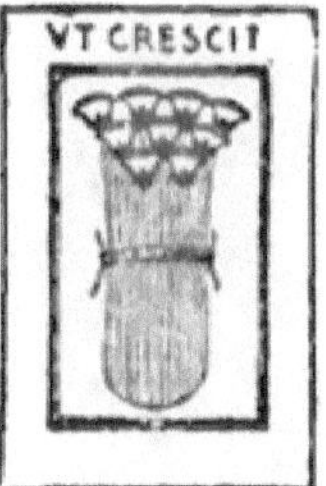

Boston, New York and London

MDCCCXCVIII

To Alice

IN LOVING REMEMBRANCE OF
OLD DAYS AT ENGLEWOOD

Contents

List of Illustrations

ix

Ye Lyttle Salem Maide

Chapter I

A Meeting in the Forest

OVER two centuries ago a little Puritan maiden might have been seen passing along the Indian path which led from out Salem Town to her home. It was near the close of day. The solemn twilight of the great primeval forest was beginning to fall. But the little maid tripped lightly on, unawed, untroubled. From underneath her snowy linen cap, with its stiffly starched ear-flaps, hung the braid of her hair, several shades more golden than the hue of her gown. Over one arm she carried her woollen stockings and buckled shoon.

A man, seated near the path on the trunk of a fallen tree of such gigantic girth that his feet swung off the ground, although he was a person of no inconsiderable size, hailed her as she neared him. "Where do you wend your way in such hasty fashion, little mistress?"

She paused and bobbed him a very fine courtesy, such as she had been taught in the Dame School, judging him to be an important personage by reason of his sword with its jewelled hilt and his plumed hat. "I be sorely hungered, good sir," she replied, "and I ken that Goody Higgins has a bowl o' porridge piping hot for me in the chimney corner." Her dimpled face grew grave; her eyelids fell. "When one for a grievous sin," she added humbly, "has stood from early morn till set o' sun on a block o' wood beside the town-pump, and has had naught to eat in all that time, one hungers much."

"And would they put a maid like you up for public punishment?" cried the Cavalier. "By my faith, these Puritans permit no children. They would have them saints, lisping brimstone and wrestling with Satan!"

"Hush, hush!" cried the little maid, affrighted. "Ye must not say that word lest the Devil answer to his name." She pointed to where the sunset glimmered red behind the trees. "Do ye not ken that when the sun be set, the witches ride on broomsticks? After dark all good children stay in the house."

"Ho, ho!" laughed the stranger; "and have you a law that witches must not ride on broomsticks? You Puritans had best be wary lest they ride your nags to death at night and you take away their broom-sticks."

"Ay," assented the maid. "Old Goody Jones is to be hanged for witchery this day week. One morn, who should find his nag steaming, flecked with foam, its mane plaited to make the bridle, but our good Neighbour Root. When I heard tell o' it, I cut across the clearing to his barn before breakfast, and with my own eyes saw the nag with its plaited mane and tail. Neigh-bour Root suspicioned who the witch was that had been riding it, but he, being an o'er-cautious man, kept a close mouth.

Well, at dawn, two days later, he jumped wide-awake all in a minute,—he had been sleeping with an eye half-cocked, as it were,—for he heard the barn door slam. He rose and lit his lantern and went out. There he saw Goody Jones hiding in a corner of the stall, her eyes shining like a cat's. When she saw he kenned her, she gave a wicked screech and flew by him in the form o' an owl. He was so afeared lest she should bewitch him, that he trembled till his red cotton nightcap fell off. It was found in the stall by our goodly magistrate in proof o' Neighbour Root's words."

The Cavalier's face grew grim. "Ay," he muttered, "the Lord will yet make these people repent the innocent blood they shed. Hark ye, little mistress, I have travelled in far countries, where they have the Black Plague and terrible diseases ye wot not of. Yet this plague of witchery is worse than all,—ay, even than the smallpox." He shrugged his shoulders and looking down at the ground, frowned and shook his head. But as he glanced up at the maid's troubled countenance, his gloom was dispelled by a sunny smile. He reached out and took her hand, and patted it between his big warm palms.

"Dear child," he said, "be not afeared of witches, but bethink yourself to keep so fair and shining a conscience that Satan and his hags who work by the powers of darkness cannot approach you. We have a play-actor in England, a Merry Andrew of the town, a slender fellow withal, yet possessed of a pretty wit, for wit, my little maid, is no respecter of persons, and springs here and there, like as one rose grows in the Queen's garden and another twines 'round the doorway of the poor. Well, this fellow has written that, 'far as a little candle throws its beams, so shines a good deed in a naughty world.' Many a time have I catched myself smiling at the jingle, for it minds me of how all good children are just so many little candles shining out into the black night of this evil world. When you are older grown you will perceive that I spake true words. Still, regarding witches, I would not have

you o'er bold nor frequent churchyards
by night, for there, I, myself, have seen
with these very eyes, ghosts and wraiths
pale as blue vapour standing by the graves.
And at cockcrow they have flown away."
He released her hand. "Come now," he
said lightly, "you have not told me why
you were made to stand on a block of
wood all day."

"Good sir," she replied, "my punishment was none too heavy, for my heart
had grown carnal and adrift from God, and
the follies and vanities o' youth had taken
hold on me. It happed in this wise.
Goodwife Higgins, who keeps our home
since my dear mother went to God, be
forever sweethearting me because I mind
her o' her own little girl who died o' the
smallpox. So she made me this fair silken
gown out o' her wedding-silk brought from
England. Ye can feel for yourself, good
sir, if ye like, that it be all silk without a thread o' cotton in it. Now, Abigail Brewster, whose father be a godly man,
told him that when I passed her going to
meeting last Sabbath morn, I switched my

fair silken gown so that it rustled in an offensive manner in her ears. So the constable came after me, and I was prosecuted in court for wearing silk in an odious manner. The Judge sentenced me to stand all day on the block, near the town-pump, exposed to public gaze in my fine raiment. Also, he did look at me o'er his spectacles in a most awesome, stern, and righteous fashion, for he said I 'drew iniquity with a cord o' vanity and sin with a cart-rope.' Then he read a stretch from the Bible, warning me to repent, lest I grow like those who 'walk with outstretched necks, mincing as they go.'" She sighed: "Ye ken not, sir, how weary one grows, standing on a block, blinking o' the sun, first resting on your heels, then tipping forward on your toes, and finding no ease. About the tenth hour, as I could see by the sun-dial, there comes Abigail Brewster walking with her father. When I catched sight o' him I put my hands over my face, and weeped with exceeding loud groans to show him I heartily repented my wickedness in the sight o' God.   But he, being spiritually minded at the time, had no thought for a sinner like me and went on.   Now, I was peeking out betwixt my fingers, and I saw Abigail Brewster had on her gown o' sad-coloured linsey-woolsey.   Her and me gave one another such a look!   For we were both acquainted like with the fact that that sad-coloured linsey-woolsey petticoat and sacque were her meeting-house clothes, her father, as I telled ye, having no patience for the follies o' dress.   Beshrew me, sir," added the little maid, timidly, "but I cannot refrain from admiring your immoderate great sleeves with the watchet-blue tiffany peeping through the slashes."

"Sit you down beside me, little mistress," said the Cavalier, "I would ask a question of you.   Ho, ho, you are afeared of witches!   Why, see the sunset still glimmers red.   Have you not a wee bit of time for me, who am in sore perplexity and distress?"

"Nay, nay, good sir," she rejoined sweetly, "I be no afeared o' witches when I can assist a soul in sore distress, for as ye telled me, a witch cannot come near one who be on a good errand."

She climbed up on the trunk and seated herself beside him, swinging her sturdy, bare feet beside his great high boots.

"Can you keep a close mouth, mistress?" asked the Cavalier.

She nodded. Irresistibly, as her companion remained silent a moment in deep thought, her fingers went out and stroked his velvet sleeve. She sighed blissfully and folded her hands in her lap.

"I was told by a countryman up the road that there is a house in your town which has been recently taken by a stranger. 'Tis a house, I am informed, with many gables and dormer windows." The speaker glanced sharply at his companion. "Do you hap to know the place?"

"Yea, good sir," she replied eagerly; "the gossips say it be a marvel with its fine furnishings, though none o' the goodwives have so much as put their noses inside the door, the master being a stern, unsocial body. But the Moorish wench who keeps his home has blabbed o' Turkey covers

and velvet stool cushions.   Ye should
hear tell — ”

“ What sort of looks has this fine gentleman,” interrupted the Cavalier; “ is he of
lean, sour countenance — ”

She nodded.

“ Crafty-eyed, tall — ”

“ Nay, not so tall,” she broke in; “ about
as ye be in height, but not so great girth
’round the middle.   The children all run
from him when he strolls out at even-tide,
tapping with his stick, and frowning.   Our
magistrate and minister hold him in great
respect as one o’ wit and learning, with
mickle gold from foreign parts.   The
naughty boys call him Old Ruddy-Beard,
for aught ye can see o’ his face be the tip
o’ his long nose ’neath the brim o’ his
beaver-hat and his red beard lying on
his white ruff.   Also he wears a cape o’
sable velvet, and he be honoured with a
title, being called Sir Jonathan Jamieson.”

During her description the Cavalier had
nodded several times, and when she finished, his face was not good to look at.

His eyes, which had been so genial, were now cold and shining as his sword.

"Have I found you at last, oh mine enemy," he exulted, "at last, at last?"

Thus he muttered and talked to himself, and his smile was not pleasant to see. Glancing at the little maid, he perceived she was startled and shrank from him. He patted her shoulder.

"Now, hark ye, mistress," he whispered, "when next you pass this man, say softly these words to greet his ears alone: 'The King sends for his black powder.'"

"Perchance he will think me a witch and I say such strange words to him," she answered, drawing away; "some say no one be more afeared o' witches than he."

The Cavalier flung back his head. His laughter rang out scornfully. "Ho, ho," he mocked, "afeared of witches, lest they carry off his black heart! He be indeed a lily-livered scoundrel! Ay, care not how much you do fright him. At first he will doubtless pretend not to hear you, still I should not be surprised and he pause and demand where you heard such words, but you must say naught of all this, e'en though he torment you with much questioning. I am on my way now to Boston Town. In a few days I shall return." He tapped her arm. "Ay, I shall return in state, in state, next time, little mistress. Meanwhile, you must keep faith with me. Let him not suspicion this meeting in the forest with me." He bent his head and whispered several sentences in her ear.

"Good sir," said the little maid, solemnly, when he had finished, "my King be next to God and I will keep the faith. But now and ye will be pleased to excuse me, as it be past the supper hour, I will hasten home." Saying which, she slipped down from the trunk of the tree and bobbed him a courtesy.

"Nay, not so fast, not so fast away," he cried. "I would show you a picture of my sweetest daughter, Elizabeth, of whom you mind me, giving me a great heart-sickness for her bonny face far across the seas in Merry England." From inside his doublet he drew forth a locket, swung on a slender gold chain, and opened it. Within was a miniature on ivory of a young girl in court dress, with dark curls falling about a face which smiled back at them in the soft twilight.

"She be good to look upon and has a comely smile, I wot," said the little Puritan maid; "haps it she has seen as many summers as I, who be turned fourteen and for a year past a teacher in the Dame School."

"Sixteen summers has she lived," answered the Cavalier. "Eftsoons, she will count in gloomier fashion, for with years come woes and we say so many winters have we known. But how comes it you are a teacher in the Dame School?"

"A fair and flowing hand I write," she replied, "though I be no great for spelling. My father has instilled a deal o' learning into my pate, but I be not puffed up with vanity on that account."

"'Tis well," said the Cavalier; "I like not an unread maid. Neither do I fancy one too much learned." He glanced again at the miniature. From smiling he fell to sighing. "Into what great girls do our daughters grow," he murmured; "but yesterday, methinks, I dandled her on my knee and sang her nursery rhymes." He opened a leathern bag strapped around his waist. Within it the little maid caught a glimpse of a gleaming array of knives both large and small. This quite startled her.

"Where did I put them?" he frowned; "but wait, but wait —" He felt in his pockets, and at last drew forth a chain of gold beads wrapped in silk. "My Elizabeth would give you these were she here," he said, "but she is far across the seas."

Rising, he bent and patted the little maid's cheek. "Take these beads, dear child, and forget not what I telled you, while I am gone to Boston Town. Yet, wait, what is your name?"

"Deliverance Wentworth," she answered. With confidence inspired anew by the kindly face, she added, "I have a brother in Boston Town, who be a Fellow o' Harvard. Should ye hap to cross his path, might ye be pleased to give him my dutiful love? He be all for learning,

and carries a mighty head on young
shoulders."

Then with another courtesy she turned
and fled fearfully along the path, for the
red of the sunset had vanished.

Far, far above her gleamed two or three
pale silver stars. The gloom of twilight
was rising thickly in the forest. Bushes
stretched out goblin arms to her as she
passed them. The rustling leaves were the
whisperings of wizards, beseeching her to
come to them. A distant stump was a witch
bending over to gather poisonous herbs.

At last she reached her home. A
flower-bordered walk led to the door.
The yard was shut in by a low stone
wall. The afterglow, still lingering on the
peaked gables of the house, was reflected
in the diamond-paned windows and on
the knocker on the front door. There
was no sign of life. Save for the spotless
neatness which marked all, the place had
a sombre and uninhabitable air, as if the
forest, pressing so closely upon the modest
farmstead, flung over it somewhat of its
own gloom and sadness.

Deliverance hesitated a moment at the gate. Her fear of the witches was great, but — she glanced at the gold beads.

"I will say a prayer all the way," she murmured, and ran swiftly along the path a goodly distance, then crossed a belt of woods, pausing neither in running nor in prayerful words, until she reached a hollow oak. In it Deliverance placed the beads wrapped in their bit of silk.

"For," she reasoned, "if father, though I be no so afeared o' father, but if Goodwife Higgins set her sharp eyes on them, I should have a most awesome, weary time with her trying to find out where I got them."

She was not far from the sea and she could see the tide coming in, a line of silver light breaking into foam. Passing along the path which led to Boston Town, she saw the portly figure of the Cavalier, the rich colours of his dress faintly to be descried. An Indian guide had joined him. Both men were on foot. Deliverance, forgetful of the witches, the darkening night, watched the travellers as long as she could see them against the silver sea. At a fordways the Cavalier paused, and the Indian stooped and took him on his back. This glimpse of her merry acquaintance, being thus carried picka-pack across the stream, was the last glimpse she had of him for many days to follow. Once she thought he waved his hand to her as he turned his head and glanced behind him. In this she was mistaken. He could not have seen the demure figure of the little Puritan maiden, standing in the deep dusk of the forest edge.

c

Chapter II

Sir Jonathan's Warning

ALTHOUGH it was an evening in early June, the salt breeze blowing damp and cold from off the sea made Master Wentworth's kitchen, with its cheerful fire, an agreeable place for the goodwives of the village to gather with their knitting after supper.

Goodwife Higgins, seated at her spinning-wheel, made but brief replies to the comments of her guests upon the forward behaviour of her foster-child Deliverance. Yet her glance was ever cast anxiously toward the door, swung half-open lest the room should become too warm.

"I trow the naughty baggage deserved correction to put to such ungodly use the fair silk ye gave her," remarked one portly dame. "Goody Dennison says as it was your standing-up gown ye brought from England to be wed in."

"Ay," said Goodwife Higgins, grimly. Her face lighted as she spoke, for the door was flung wide and the little maid of whom they spoke entered, breathless with running.

"It be time ye were in," frowned Goodwife Higgins, a note of relief in her sharp tone. "I gan to think a witch had catched ye."

"Come, come, child, stand out and let us see those fine feathers which have filled your foolish pate with vanity," cried Goody Dennison.

Deliverance sighed profoundly. "I do repent deeply that iniquity and vanity should have filled my carnal heart because o' this fair gown o' silk. Ye can feel for yourself and ye like, Goody Dennison, there be no thread o' cotton in it."

As she spoke she glanced out of the corners of her downcast eyes at a little, rosy, freckled girl, who sat at her mother's side, knitting, but who did not look up, keeping her sleek brown head bent resolutely over the half-finished stocking.

"Have ye had aught to eat, child?" asked Goodwife Higgins.

Deliverance shook her head.

"And ye would go off with but a sup o' milk for breakfast," scolded the good-wife, as she rose and stirred the porridge she had saved. "Sit ye down by Abigail, and I will bring ye summat nourishing."

Now, Deliverance had stood long in the hot sun with naught to eat, and this and her long walk so weighed upon her that suddenly she grew pale and sank to the floor.

"Dear Goody," she murmured faintly, "the Lord has struck my carnal heart with the bolt o' His righteous anger, for I wax ill."

That the welfare, if not the pleasure, of their children lay very close to the hearts of the Puritans, was shown by the manner in which the goodwives, who had greeted Deliverance with all due severity, dropped their knitting and gathered hastily around her.

"It be too long a sentence for a grow-ing child, and it behooves us who are

mothers to tell our godly magistrate so,"
grumbled one hard-featured dame.

"Dear child," murmured a rosy-cheeked
young wife, who had put her baby down to
assist Deliverance, " here be a sugar-plum
I brought ye. We must have remembrance, gossips," she added, "that her
mother has long been dead, though
Goodwife Higgins cares for her and that
be well, Master Wentworth being a
dreamer. Ye ken, gossips, I say it with
no malice, the house might go to rack
and ruin, for aught he would care, with
his nose ever in the still-room."

"Best put the child in the chimney-
corner where it be warm," suggested
Goody Dennison; "beshrew me, gossips,
the damp o' these raw spring nights chills
the marrow in your bones more than the
frosts o' winter."

So Deliverance was seated on a stool
next to Abigail Brewster, with Goodwife
Higgins' apron tied around her neck, a
pewter bowl of steaming hasty-pudding in
her lap, a mug of milk conveniently near.

The goodwives, their attention taken

from the little maid, turned their conversation upon witchcraft, and as they talked, sturdy voices shook and florid faces blanched at every gust of wind in the chimney.

"Abigail," whispered Deliverance, "did ye e'er clap eyes on Goody Jones sith she became a witch?"

"Never," answered Abigail. "Father told me to run lest she give me the malignant touch. Oh dear, I have counted my stitches wrong."

The humming of Goodwife Higgins' spinning-wheel made a musical accompaniment to all that was said. And the firelight dancing over the spinner's ruddy face and buxom figure made of her a pleasant picture as she guided the thread, her busy foot on the treadle.

Ah, what tales were told around the fireplace of the New England kitchen where centred all homely cheer and comfort, and the gossips' tongues wagged fast as the glancing knitting-needles flashed! High in the yawning chimney, from ledge to ledge, stretched the great lugpole, made from green wood that it might not catch fire. From it swung on hooks the pots and kettles used in cooking. Bright andirons reflected the dancing flames and on either side were the settles. From the heavy rafters were festooned strings of dried fruit, small yellow and green squashes, scarlet peppers. Sand was scattered over the floor. Darkness, banished by the fire-light, lurked in the far corners of the room.

Abigail and Deliverance, to all outward appearance absorbed in each other's society, were none the less listening with ears wide open to whatever was said. Near them sat young wife Tucker that her baby might share the warmth of the fire. It lay on her lap, its little red hands curled up, the lashes of its closed eyes sweeping its cheeks. A typical Puritan baby was this, duly baptized and given to God. A wadded hood of gray silk was worn closely on its head, its gown, short-sleeved and low-necked, was of coarse linen bleached in the sun and smelling sweetly of lavender. The young wife tilted it gently on her knees, crooning psalms if it appeared to be waking, the while her ever busy hands were knitting above it. Once she paused to touch the round cheek fondly with her finger.

"Ye were most fortunate, Dame Tucker," said one of the gossips, observing the tender motion, "to get him back again."

"Ay," answered the young wife, "the Lord was merciful to the goodman and myself. Ne'er shall I cease to have remembrance o' that wicked morn. I waked early and saw a woman standing by the cradle. 'In God's name, what come you for?' I cried, and thereat she vanished. I rose; O woeful sight these eyes beheld! The witches had taken away my babe and put in its stead a changeling." The young wife shuddered, and dropped her knitting to clasp her baby to her breast. "Long had I been feared o' such an evil and ne'er oped my eyes at morn save with fear lest the dread come true. Ye ken, gossips, a witch likes best a first bairn. There the changeling lay in my baby's crib, a puny, fretful, crying wean, purple o' lips and white o' cheeks. Quick the goodman went out and got me five eggs from the black hen, and we burnt the shells and fried the yolks, and with a jar o' honey (for a witch has a sweet tooth) put the relishes where she might find them and be pacified. She took them not. All that day and the next I wept sorely. Yet with rich milk I fed the fretting wean, feeling pity for it in my heart though it was against me to hush it to sleep in my arms. The night o' the second day the goodman slept heavily, for he was sore o' heart an' weary. But the changeling would not hush its wailing, so I rose and rocked it until worn out by much grief I fell asleep, my head resting on the hood o' the crib. When I oped my eyes in the darkness the crying was like that o' my own babe. I hushed my breath to listen.

" Quick I got a tallow dip and lighted it for to see what was in the crib. I fell on my knees and prayed. The witches had brought back my bairn, and taken their fretting wean away."

"How looked it?" asked Deliverance, eagerly. She never wearied hearing of the changeling, and her interest was as fresh at the third telling of the story as at the first. And, although under most circumstances she would have been chidden for speaking out before her elders, she escaped this time, so interested were the goodwives in the tale.

"Full peaked and wan it looked," answered the young wife, solemnly, "and blue it was from hunger and cold, for no witches' food will nourish a baptized child."

"I should have liked to see where the witches took it, shouldn't ye?" whispered Abigail to Deliverance.

"Abigail," said Deliverance, in a cautious whisper, although the humming of the spinning-wheel almost drowned her voice, "if ye will be pleasant-mouthed and not run tittle-tattling upon me again, perchance I will tell ye summat, only it would make your eyes pop out o' your head. Ye be that simple-minded, Abigail! And I might show ye summat too, only I misdoubt ye have a carnal heart which longs too much on things that glitter. Here, ye can bite off the end o' my sugar-plum. Now, whisper no word o' what I tell ye," putting her mouth to the other's ear, " I be on a service for his majesty, King George."

A door leading from an inner room into the kitchen opened and a man came out. He was tall and hollow-chested and stooped slightly. His flaxen wig, parted in the centre, fell to his shoulders on either side of his hatchet-shaped face. He had mild blue eyes. His presence diffused faint odours of herbs and dried flowers and fragrance of scented oils. This sweet atmosphere, surrounding him wherever he went, heralded his presence often before he appeared.

" Has Deliverance returned, Goodwife Higgins?" he asked. " I need her to find me the yarrow."

" And do ye think I would not have the child housed at this hour o' night?" queried the goodwife, sharply; " your father needs ye, Deliverance. Ye ken, gossips," she added in a softened voice, as Master Wentworth retired, "that the poor man has no notion o' what be practicable. It be fair exasperating to a decent, well-providing body to care for him."

Deliverance hastily set the porridge bowl on the hearth, and followed her father into the still-room.

Next to the kitchen the still-room was the most important one in the house. Here were kept all preserves and liquors, candied fruits and spices. From the rafters swung bunches of dried herbs, the gathering and arrangement of which was Deliverance's especial duty. From early spring until Indian summer did she work to make these precious stores. With the melting of the snows, when the Indian women boiled the sweet waters of the maple, she went forth to hunt for wintergreen. Together she and her father gathered slippery-elm and sassafras bark. Then, green, fragrant, wholesome, appeared the mints. Also there were mysterious herbs which grew in graveyards and must be culled only at midnight.

And there was the blessed thistle, which no good child ever plucked before she sang the verse : —

> " Hail, to thee, holy herb,
>   Growing in the ground,
> On the Mount of Calvarie,
>   First wert thou found.
> Thou art good for many a grief
>   And healest many a wound,
> In the name of Sweet Jesu,
>   I lift thee from the ground."

And there were saffron, witch-hazel, rue, shepherd's-purse, and bloody-dock, not to mention the yearly store of catnip put away for her kitten.

Master Wentworth swung her up on his shoulder so she could reach the rafters.

" The yarrow be tied fifth bunch on the further beam, father," she said ; "there, ye have stopped right under it."

Her small fingers quickly untied the string and the great bunch of yarrow was in her arms as her father set her down. He handed her a mortar bowl and pestle.

" Seat yourself, Deliverance," he said, " and pound this into a paste for me."

Vigorously Deliverance pounded, anxious to return to Abigail.

The room was damp and chilly. No heat came in from the kitchen for the door was closed, but the little Puritan maiden was inured to the cold and minded it not. The soft light that filled the room was given by three dipped candles made from the fragrant bayberry wax. This wax was of a pale green, almost transparent colour, and gave forth a pleasant fragrance when snuffed. An hour-glass was placed behind one of the candles that the light might pass through the running sands and enable one to read the time at a glance. At his table as he worked, her father's shadow was flung grotesquely on the wall, now high, now low. Into the serene silence the sound of Deliverance's pounding broke with muffled regularity.

" I am telled, Master Wentworth," said a harsh voice, " that your dear and only daughter, Deliverance, be given o'er to vanity. Methinks, the magistrate awarded her too light a sentence for her idle flauntings. As I did chance to meet him at the tavern, at the nooning-hour, I took it upon myself to tell him, humbly, however, and in no spirit of criticism, that too great a leniency accomplishes much evil."

Deliverance fairly jumped, so startled was she by the unexpected voice. Now for the first time she perceived a gentleman, in a sable cape, his booted legs crossed, and his arms folded on his breast, as he sat in the further corner of the room. One side of his face was hidden from view by the illuminated hour-glass, but the light of the concealed candle cast so soft and brilliant a glow over his figure that she was amazed at not having seen him before. His red beard rested on the white ruff around his neck. She could see but the tip of his long nose beneath his steeple-crowned hat. Yet she felt the gaze of those shadowed eyes fixed upon her piercingly. None other than Sir Jonathan Jamieson was he, of whom the stranger in the forest had made inquiry.

As she remembered the words she was commissioned to say to this man, her heart throbbed fast with fear. She ceased pounding. Silently she prayed for courage to keep her promise and to serve her King.

At Sir Jonathan's words, Master Wentworth glanced up with a vague smile, having barely caught the drift of them.

"Ah, yes," he said, "women are prone to care for fol-de-rols. Still, I have seen fine dandies in our sex. I am minded of my little girl's dear mother, who never could abide this bleak country and our sad Puritan ways, sickening for longing of green old England." He sighed. "Yet," he added hastily, "I criticise not our godly magistrate's desire to crush out folly." He turned and peered into the mortar bowl. "You are slow at getting that smooth, daughter."

Deliverance commenced pounding again hurriedly. Although she looked straight into the bowl she could see plainly that stern figure in the further corner, the yellow candle-light touching brilliantly the red beard and white ruff. She trembled and doubted her courage to give him the message.

"Take care lest you harbour a witch
in yonder girl"

But there was staunch stuff in this little Puritan maid, and as her father's guest rose to depart and was about to pass her on his way to the door, she looked up.

"Good sir," she whispered, "the King sends for his black powder."

Thereat Sir Jonathan jumped, and his jaw fell as if he had been dealt an unexpected blow. He looked down at her as if he beheld a much more terrible sight than a little maid, whose knees knocked together with trembling so that the mortar bowl danced in her lap, and whose frightened blue eyes never left his face in their fascinated stare of horror at her own daring. A moment he stared back at her, then muttering, he hurried out into the kitchen and slammed the door behind him.

"Gossips," he cried harshly, "take care lest you harbour a witch in yonder girl."

With that, wrapping his cape of sable velvet around him, and with a swing of his black stick, he flung wide the kitchen door, and passed out into the night.

"Father," asked Deliverance, timidly,

"how haps it that Sir Jonathan comes this way?"

Master Wentworth answered absent-mindedly, "What, daughter, you are concerned about Sir Jonathan. Yes, yes, run and get him a mug of sweet sack and you like. Never let it be said I sent from my door rich or poor, without offering him cheer."

"Nay, father," she protested, "I but asked —"

"Let me see," murmured Master Wentworth; "to eight ounces of orris root, add powdered cuttle-bone of like quantity, a gill of orange-flower water. What said you, child," interrupting himself, "a mug of sack for Sir Jonathan. Run quickly and offer it to him lest he be gone."

Reluctantly, Deliverance opened the door and stepped out into the kitchen. Sir Jonathan had been gone several moments. She was astonished to see the goodwives had risen and were huddled together in a scared group with blanched faces, all save Goodwife Higgins, who stood alone at her spinning-wheel. The eyes of all were directed toward the still-room. The baby, clutched tightly to its fearful young mother's breast, wailed piteously.

Deliverance, abashed although she knew not why, paused when half-way across the room.

"Look ye, gossips," cried one, "look at the glint o' her een."

To these Puritan dames the extreme beauty which the solitary childish figure acquired in the firelight was diabolical. The reflection of the dancing flames made a radiant nimbus of her fair, disordered hair, and brought out the yellow sheen in the silken gown. Her lips were scarlet, her cheeks glowed, while her soft eyes, wondrously blue and clear, glanced round the circle of faces. Before that innocent and astonished gaze, first one person and then another of the group cowered and shrank, muttering a prayer.

Through the door, swung open by the wind, swept a terrible gust, and with it passed in something soft, black, fluttering, which circled three times around the room, each time drawing nearer to Deliverance, until at last it dropped and fastened itself to her hair.

Shrieking, the women broke from each other, and ran from the room, all save Goodwife Higgins, who clapped her apron over her head, and fell to uttering loud groans.

Master Wentworth came out from the still-room, a bunch of yarrow under one arm, and holding the mortar bowl.

"What ungodly racket is this?" he asked. "Is a man to find no peace in his own house?"

Upon hearing his voice, Goodwife Higgins' fright somewhat abated. She drew down her apron, and pointed speechlessly to Deliverance who was rigid with terror.

"Lord bless us!" cried the goodman. "Have you no wits at all, woman?" He laid the bowl on the table, unconsciously letting the herbs slip to the floor, and hastened to Deliverance's assistance.

"You have catched a bird, daughter, but no singing-bird, only a loathsome bat. Why, Deliverance, weep not. My little Deliverance, there is naught to be frightened at. 'Tis a very pitiful thing," he continued, lapsing into his musing tone, while his long fingers drew the fair hair from the bat's claws with much deftness, "how some poor, pitiful creatures be made with nothing for to win them grace and kind looks, only a hideous body, so that silly women scatter like as a viper had come amongst them; and yet, even the vipers and toads have jewelled eyes, did one but look for them."

He crossed the room, and put the bat outside, then bolted the door for the night.

"I am minded of your dear mother, daughter," he said, a tender smile on his face; "she was just so silly about some poor, pitiful creature which had no fine looks for to win it smiles. But she was ay bonny to the poor, Deliverance, and has weeped o'er many a soul in distress."

Chapter III

The Yellow Bird

GOODWIFE HIGGINS, who kept the home for the little maid and her father, rose early the next day before the sun was up. The soft light of dawn filled the air; the eastern sky was breaking rosily. A moment, she stood in the doorway, inhaling with delight the fresh, delicious air, noting how the dew lay white as hoar-frost on the grass. She made the fire and put the kettle on to boil, filling it first with water from the spring. Then she went to Deliverance's room to awaken her, loath to do so, for she felt the little maid had become very weary the previous day. To her surprise she found the small hooded bed empty.

"The dear child," smiled the goodwife, "she has gone to gather strawberries for her father's breakfast. She repents, I perceive, her unchastened heart, and seeks to pleasure me by an o'er amount o' promptness."

She turned to fling back the covers of the bed that they might air properly. This, however, had already been done. On the window-ledge a little yellow bird sat preening its feathers. It looked at her with its bright, black eyes and continued its dainty toilet undisturbed. Now, this was strange, for as every one knew, the wild canary was a shy bird and flew away at the least approach. The goodwife grew pale, for she feared she was in the presence of a witch, knowing that witches often took upon themselves the forms of yellow birds, that they might by such an innocent and harmless seeming, accomplish much evil among unsuspecting persons. She tiptoed out of the room, and returned with her Bible as a protection against any spell the witch might cast upon her.

"Ye wicked one," she cried, and her voice shook, "ye who have given yourself over from God to the Devil, get ye gone from this godly house!"

At these words the bird flew away, proving it beyond doubt to be possessed by an evil spirit, for it is known that a witch cannot bear to hear the name of the Lord. The goodwife was yet more affrighted to see the bird fly in the woods in the direction in which the strawberry patch lay. There Deliverance probably was. What power could avail against the witch casting a malignant spell upon her? She leaned out of the window, calling, —

"Deliverance, Deliverance, come into the house! There be a witch abroad. Deliverance, oh, Deliverance!"

Several moments passed. At last to her anxious gaze appeared Deliverance, tripping out of the green woods from the direction in which the bird had flown. She was attired in her tiffany gown, and there was that about the yellow sheen of the fair silk and the long braid of her yellow hair which made her seem like the yellow bird in human form. The first rays of the sun struck aslant her head. She was singing, and as she sang she smiled. She could not have gone to gather berries, for she carried neither basket nor dish. It was evident she had not heard her name called, for she paused startled and abashed, and the singing words died on her lips, when she saw the dame leaning out of the window.

"Deliverance, ye naughty baggage," cried the goodwife, sharply, "where have ye been and what for have ye on your gown o' tiffany?"

The words were stern, but her heart was beating like to break and throbbed in unison with Sir Jonathan's warning the previous night. "Gossips, take care lest you harbour a witch in yonder girl." She hurried to the kitchen door to meet Deliverance. As the little maid shamefacedly crossed the threshold she raised her hand to strike her, but dropped it to her side and shook her head, for in her heart she said sadly, "And gin ye be a witch, child, sore will be your punishment and my hand shall add no blow." For she was minded of her own little girl who had died of the smallpox so many years ago. She prepared the breakfast with more bustle and noise than usual, as was her wont when disturbed.

Deliverance, greatly mortified at having been detected and wondering why she was not questioned, went to her room and put on her linsey-woolsey petticoat and sacque.

When she came out to lay the table, to her surprise, Goodwife Higgins spoke her gently. "Go, child, and call your father, for the Indian bread be right crusty and brown and the bacon crisp."

Deliverance opened the still-room door. Master Wentworth, attired in his morning-gown, was preparing his work for the day. He was celebrated in Boston Town for his beauty and honey waters as well as for his diet-drinks. Recently, he had had a large order from the Governor's lady — who had many vanities and was very fine indeed — for balls of sweet gums and oils, which, wrapped in geranium leaves, were to be burned on coals to perfume the room.

This morning no accustomed sweet odour greeted Deliverance. Pungent, disagreeable fumes rose from the bowl over which her father bent.   So absorbed was he in this experiment that he did not answer until she had called him several times.

Then he greeted her kindly and the two walked out to breakfast. Goodwife Higgins watched Deliverance narrowly while grace was said and her heart grew lighter to behold the little maid listen devoutly, her head humbly bowed, as she said "amen" with fervour. Nevertheless, Sir Jonathan's words rang in the dame's ears all day : " Gossips, take care lest you harbour a witch in yonder girl."

Even the cream was bewitched. The butter would not come until she had heated a horseshoe red-hot and hung it over the churn. Also, three times a mouse ran across the floor.

Deliverance hurried through her morning chores, anxious to reach the town's highway before school called, that she might see the judges go riding by to court, then being held in Salem. A celebrated trial of witches was going on. In the front yard she found Goodwife Higgins weeding the flower-bed.

"Be a good child, Deliverance," said the dame, looking up with troubled face, for she was much perplexed over the unseemly conduct of the little maid.

"Might ye be pleased to kiss me before I go?" asked Deliverance, putting up her cheek.

The goodwife barely touched her lips to the soft cheek, having a secret fear lest the little maid were in communion with evil spirits. Her heart was so full of grief that her eyes filled with tears, and she could scarce see whether she were pulling up weeds or flowers.

As soon as Deliverance had made the turn of the road and was beyond the goodwife's vision, she began to run in her anxiety to reach the town's highway and see the reverend judges go riding by. The Dame School lay over half-way to town, facing the road, but she planned to make a cut through the forest back of the building, that she might not be observed by any scholars going early to school. To her disappointment, these happy plans were set at naught by hearing the conch-shell blown to call the children in. In her haste she had failed to consult the hour-glass before leaving home. She was so far away as to be late even as it was, and she did not dare be any later. She stamped her foot with vexation. The school door was closed when she reached it, out of breath, cross, and flurried. She raised the knocker and rapped. A prim little girl opened the door. Prayers had already been said and Dame Grundle had called the first class in knitting.

Deliverance courtesied low to the dame, who kept the large room with the older scholars. There were four rows of benches filled with precise little girls. The class in knitting was learning the fox-and-geese pattern, a most fashionable and difficult stitch, new from Boston Town. In this class was Abigail Brewster.

Deliverance opened the door into the smaller room. At her entrance soft whispers and gurgles of laughter ceased. She had twelve scholars, seven girls and five boys, the boys seated on the bench back of the girls.

The little girls were exact miniatures of the larger scholars in Dame Grundle's room. Each of them held a posy for her teacher, the frail wild flowers already wilting. The boys, devoid of any such sentiment, were twisting, wriggling, and whispering. Typical Puritan boys were they with cropped heads, attired in homespun small-clothes, their bare feet and legs tanned and scratched.

Deliverance made all an elaborate courtesy.

They slipped down from the benches, the girls bobbing and the boys ducking their heads, in such haste that two of them knocked together and commenced quarrelling. Deliverance, with a vigorous shake of each small culprit, put them at opposite ends of the bench. The first task was the study of the alphabet. A buzz of whispering voices arose as the children conned their letters from books made of two sheets of horn: on one side the alphabet was printed and on the other the Lord's Prayer. The humming of the little voices over their A, B, C's made a pleasant accompaniment to their teacher's thought, who, with every stitch in the sampler she was embroidering, wove in a vision of herself in a crimson velvet gown and stomacher worked with gold thread, such as were worn by the little court lady, the Cavalier's sweetest daughter. Growing conscious of a disturbance in class she looked up.

"Stability Williams," she said sternly, "can ye no sit still without jerking around like as your head was loosed?"

Stability's tears flowed copiously at the reproof.

"Please, ma'am," spoke up Hannah Sears, "he's been pulling o' her hair."

Deliverance's sharp eyes spied the guilty offender.

"Ebenezer Gibbs," said she, "stop your wickedness, and as for ye, Stability Williams, cease your idle soughing."

For awhile all was quiet. Then, there broke forth a muffled sob from Stability, followed by an irrepressible giggle from the boys. Deliverance stepped down from the platform and rapped

Ebenezer Gibbs' head smartly with her thimble.

"Ye rude and ill-mannered boy," she cried; "have ye no shame to be pulling Stability Williams' hair and inticing others to laugh at your evil doings? Ye can just come along now and stand in the crying-corner."

The crying-corner was the place where the children stood to weep after they had been punished. Pathetic record of childish grief was this corner, the pine boards black with the imprint of small grimy fingers and spotted with tears from little wet faces. Doubtless Deliverance rapped the offender more severely than she intended, for he wept steadily. Although she knew he deserved the reproof, his crying smote her heart sorely.

"Ebenezer Gibbs," she said, after a while, "when ye think ye have weeped sufficient long, ye can take your seat."

But he continued to weep and sniffle the entire morning, not even ceasing when his companions had their resting-minute. The day was quite spoiled for Deliverance by the sight of the tiny figure with the cropped head pressed close in the corner, as the culprit rested first on one foot and then the other.

Altogether she was very glad when Dame Grundle rang the bell for dismissal, and she could put on the children's things and conduct them home. It was a pleasant walk to town through the woods. Deliverance, at the head of her little procession, always entered the village at an angle to pass the meeting-house where all important news was given forth and public gatherings held. The great front door faced the highway and was the town bulletin board. Sometimes a constable was stationed near by to read the message aloud to the unlettered. A chilling wind swept down the road this morning as Deliverance and her following drew near.

Inside the meeting-house the great witch-trial was still in session. A large crowd, which could not be accommodated inside, thronged the steps and peered in through the windows. The sun which had risen so brightly, had disappeared.

The gray sky, the raw air, hung gloomily over the scene, wherein the sad-coloured garments of the gentlefolk made a background for the bright bodices of the goodwives, and the red, green, and blue doublets of the yeomen. Soldiers mingled with the throng. So much noise had disturbed the court that the great door had been ordered closed. On the upper panels wolves' heads (nailed by hunters in proof of their success that they might receive the bounty), with grinning fangs and blood trickling to the steps, looked down upon the people.

The children with Deliverance grew frightened and clutched at her dress, trying to drag her away, but she, eager to hear whatever news there was, silenced them peremptorily.

Suddenly she heard a strange sound. Glancing down she beheld one of her scholars, crawling on his hands and knees, mewing like a cat. Another child imitated this curious action, and yet another. A fourth child screamed and fell in convulsions. In a few moments the panic had spread to them all. The children were mad with terror. One little girl began barking like a dog, still another crowed like a cock, flapping her arms as though they were wings.

The crowd, disturbed by the shrill cries, turned its attention and pressed around the scene of fresh excitement. Faces of hearty women and stout men blanched.

" Even the babes be not spared," they cried ; " see, they be bewitched."

Goodwife Gibbs broke from the rest, and lifted up her little son who lay in convulsions on the dusty road. " The curse o' God be on the witch who has done this," she cried wildly ; " let her be revealed that she may be punished."

The child writhed, then grew quiet; a faint colour came back into his face. His eyelids quivered and unclosed. Deliverance called him by name, bending over him as he lay in his mother's arms. As she did so he struck her in the face, a world of terror in his eyes, screaming that she was the witch and had stuck pins in him.

"Dear Lord," cried the little maid, aghast, raising her eyes to heaven, "ye ken I but rapped his pate for sniffling and larfing in class."

But strange rumours were afloat regarding Deliverance Wentworth. Sir Jonathan's words were on every gossip's tongue : " Gossips, take care lest you harbour a witch in yonder girl."

Naturally, at the convulsed child's words, which seemed a confirmation of that warning, the good people drew away, shuddering, each man pressing against his neighbour, until they formed a circle a good distance back from the little assistant teacher of the Dame School.

Thus Deliverance stood at noonday, publicly disgraced, sobbing, with her hands over her face in the middle of the roadway ; an object of hatred and abhorrence, with the screaming children clutching at her dress, or crawling at her feet.

But suddenly her father, who, returning from his herb-gathering, had pushed his way to the edge of the crowd and perceived Deliverance, stepped out and took his daughter by the hand. He spoke sternly to those who blocked the way, so that the people parted to let them pass. Master Wentworth was a man of dignity and high repute in those parts.

As the two walked home hand in hand, Deliverance, with many tears, related the morning's events; how in some anger she had rapped Ebenezer Gibbs' head with her thimble, and how he had cried thereat.

"I am ashamed of you, Deliverance," said her father. "Have you no heart of grace that you must needs be filled with evil and violence because of the naughtiness of a little child? Moreover, if you had been discreet all this mortification had not befallen you. How many times have you been telled, daughter, not to idle on the way, ogling, gossiping, and craning your neck about for curiosity? And now we will say nothing more about it," he ended. "Only do you remember, Deliverance, that when people are given over to foolishness, and there is a witch panic, it behooves the wise to be very prudent, and to walk soberly, with shut mouth and downcast eyes, so that no man may point his finger and accuse them. Methinks Goodwife Gibbs' boy is coming down with a fever sickness. Remind me that I brew a strengthening draught for him to-night."

Chapter IV

In which Demons assault the Meeting-
house

THE Sabbath day dawned clear with
a breeze blowing soft, yet cool and
invigorating, from off the sea.

But the brightness of the day could not
lighten the hearts of the villagers, de-
pressed by the terrible witch-trials.

Master Wentworth, however, maintained a certain peace in his home, which,
lying on the outskirts of the town, was
just beyond the circle of village gossip.
Moreover, he sternly checked any tendency in Goodwife Higgins or Deliverance
to comment on the panic that was abroad.
So of all the homes in Salem his little
household knew the deepest peace on the
morn of that memorable Sabbath.

" Goodwife," he said, passing his cup
for a third serving of tea, " your Sabbath

face is full as bonny a thing to look at
and warms the heart, as much as your tea
and muffins console an empty stomach."

And the goodwife replied with some
asperity to conceal her pleasure at the
remark, for, being comely, she delighted
to be assured of the fact, "Ay, the cook's
face be bonny, and the tea be well brewed.
Ye have a flattering tongue, Master
Wentworth."

Then Master Wentworth, stirring his tea
which had a sweetening of molasses, related how, having once had a chest of tea
sent him from old England, he had por-
tioned part of it among his neighbours.
The goodwives, being ignorant of its use,
had boiled it well and flung the water
away.   But the leaves they kept and sea-
soned as greens.

Now, this little story was as delicious to
Master Wentworth as the flavour of his
tea, and being an absent-minded body,
withal possessed of a most gentle sense of
humour, he told it every Sabbath breakfast.

He continued to converse in this gentle
mood with Goodwife Higgins and Deliv-

erance, as the three wended their way to church.

Very cool and pleasant was the forest road. Now and then through the green they caught glimpses of the white turret of the meeting-house, as yet without a bell. The building was upon a hill, that travellers and hunters might be guided by a sight of it.

Often there passed them a countryman, the goodwife mounted behind her husband on a pillion. Later they would pass the horse tied to a tree and see the couple afoot far down the road. This was the custom when there was but one horse in the family. After awhile the children, carrying their shoes and stockings, would reach the horse and, as many as could, pile on the back of the much enduring nag and ride merrily the rest of the way.

Master Wentworth and his family arrived early. The watchman paced the platform above the great door, beating a drum to call the people to service. Several horses were tied to the hitching-post. Some of the people were wandering in the churchyard which stretched down the hill-slope.

Others of the sad-eyed Puritans gathered in little groups, discussing a new and terrible doctrine which had obtained currency. It was said that the gallows had been set up, not only for the guilty but for those who rebuked the superstition of witchery. The unbelievers would be made to suffer to the fullest extent of the law.

And another fearful rumour was being circulated to the effect that a renowned witch-finder of England had been sent for. He was said to discover a witch by some mark on the body, and then cause the victim to be bound hand and foot and cast into a pond. If the person floated he was pronounced guilty and straightway drawn out and hanged. But he who was innocent sank at once.

Soldiers brought from Boston Town to quell any riots that might arise, added an unusual animation to the scene. Lieutenant-Governor Stoughton and the six other judges conducting the trials, were the centre of a group of the gentry.

Deliverance and Abigail Brewster strolled among the tombstones reading their favourite epitaphs. The two little maids, having the innocent and happy hearts of childhood, had found only pleasurable excitement in the witch-panic until the morning Deliverance had been accused by her pupils. But they believed this affair had blown over and remained only a thrilling subject for conversation. Both felt the Devil had made an unsuccessful assault upon Deliverance, and, as she wrote in her diary, sought to destroy her good name with the " Malice of Hell."

During meeting Deliverance sat with Goodwife Higgins on the women's side of the building. Her father, being of the gentry, was seated in one of the front pews.

Through the unshuttered windows the sunlight streamed in broadly, and as the air grew warm one could smell the pine and rosin in the boards of the house. Pushed against the wall was the clerk's table with its plentiful ink-horn and quills.

The seven judges, each of whom had, according to his best light, condemned the guilty and let the innocent go free, during the past week, now sat in a row below the pulpit.   Doubtless each felt himself in the presence of the Great Judge of all things and, bethinking himself humbly of his own sins, prayed for mercy.

The soldiers stacked their firearms and sat in a body on the men's side of the church.   Their scarlet uniforms made an unusual amount of colour in the sober meeting-house.

The long hours dragged wearily.

Little children nodded, and their heads fell against their mothers' shoulders, or dropped into their laps.   Sometimes they were given lemon drops or sprigs of sweet herbs.   One solemn little child, weary of watching the great cobwebs swinging from the rafters, began to count aloud his alphabet, on ten moist little fingers.   He was sternly hushed.

The tithing-man ever tiptoed up and down seeking to spy some offender.   When a woman or maid grew drowsy, he brushed her chin with the end of his wand which bore a fox's tail.   But did some goodman nod, he pricked him smartly with the thorned end.

Deliverance loved the singing, and her young voice rang out sweetly as she stood holding her psalm-book, her blue eyes devoutly raised.   And the armed watchman pacing the platform above the great door, his keen glance sweeping the surrounding country for any trace of Indians or Frenchmen, joined lustily in the singing.

Many voices faltered and broke this morning.   Few families but missed some beloved face.   Over one hundred persons in the little village were in prison accused of witchery.

The minister filled his prayers with the subject of witchcraft and made the barn-like building ring with the text: " Have I not chosen you twelve, and one of you is a devil ? "

At this Goodwife Cloyse, who sat next to Deliverance, rose and left the meeting-house in displeasure.   She believed the text alluded to her sister, who was then in prison charged with having a familiar spirit.

The next day she too was cried upon and cast into prison as a witch, although a woman of purest life.

Deliverance thrilled with terror at the incident. She felt she had been seated next to a witch, and this in God's own house. Moreover she imagined a sudden pain in her right arm, and dreaded lest a spell had been cast on her.

The day which opened with so fearful an event was to end yet more ominously.

Following the sermon came the pleasant nooning-hour. The people gathered in family groups on the meeting-house steps, or sought the shade of the nearby trees and ate their lunches. The goodwives provided bountifully for the soldiers, and the judges ate with the minister and his family.

Toward the end of the nooning-hour Master Wentworth sent Deliverance to carry to Goodwife Gibbs the tea he had brewed.

"Father sends ye this, goodwife," said the little maid; "it be a strengthening draught for Ebenezer. He bids me tell ye a fever sickness has seized o' the child."

The goodwife snatched the bottle and flung it violently from her.

" Get ye gone with your brew, ye witch-maid !   No fever sickness ails my little son, but a spell ye have put upon him." She began to weep sorely.   Duty compelled her to attend meeting, the while her heart sickened that she must leave her little son in the care of a servant wench.

The gossips crowded around her in sympathy.   Dark looks were cast upon Deliverance, and muttered threats were made.   Their voices rose with their growing anger, until the minister, walking arm-in-arm with Master Wentworth, heard them and was roused to righteous indignation.

" Hush, gossips," he said sternly, " we will have no high words on the Lord's holy day, but peace and comfort and meek and contrite hearts, else we were hypocrites.   We will continue our discussion next week, Master Wentworth," he added, turning to his companion, " for the nooning-hour is done."

Master Wentworth, who was given to day-dreaming, had scarce heard the hubbub, and had not even perceived his daughter, who was standing near by. So, a serene smile on his countenance, he followed the minister into the meeting-house.

His little maid, very sorrowful at this fresh trouble which had come upon her, and not being able to attract his attention before he entered the building, wandered away into the churchyard.

That afternoon the tithing-man missed her in the congregation. So he tiptoed out of the meeting-house in search of her.

He called up softly to the watchman, —

"Take your spy-glass and search if ye see aught o' Mistress Deliverance Wentworth."

The watchman started guiltily, and leaned over the railing with such sudden show of interest that the tithing-man grew suspicious. His sharp eyes spied a faint wavering line of smoke rising from the corner of the platform. So he guessed the smoke rose from the overturned bowl of a pipe, and that the watchman had been smoking, a comfortable practice which had originated among the settlers of Virginia. Being in a good humour, he was disposed to ignore this indiscretion on the part of the watchman.

The latter had now fixed his spy-glass in the direction of the churchyard.

" I see a patch o' orange tiger-lilies far down the hillside," he announced, "and near by be a little grave grown o'er with sweetbrier.   And   there, with her head pillowed on the headstone, be Mistress Deliverance Wentworth, sound in sleep."

Thus the little maid was found by the tithing-man, and wakened and marched back to church.

As the two neared the entrance the watchman called her softly, " Hey, there, Mistress Deliverance Wentworth, what made ye fall asleep ? "

" The Devil set a snare for my feet," she answered mournfully, not inclined to attach too much blame to herself.

" Satan kens his own," said the watchman severely, quickly hiding his pipe behind him.

Now, at the moment of the disgraced little maid's entrance, a great rush of wind swept in and a timber in the rafters was blown down, reaching the floor, however, without injury to any one.

Many there were who later testified to having seen Deliverance raise her eyes just before the timber fell. These believed that she had summoned a demon, who, invisibly entering the meeting-house on the wings of the wind, had sought to destroy it.

The sky, lately so blue, grew leaden gray. So dark it became, that but few could see to read the psalms. Thunder as yet distant could be heard, and the roaring of the wind in the tree-tops, and ever in the pauses of the storm, the ominous booming of the ocean.

The watchman came inside. The tithing-man closed and bolted the great door.

The minister prayed fervently for mercy. None present but believed that an assault of the demons upon God's house was about to be made.

The rain began to fall heavily, beating

in at places through the rafters.   Flashes of lightning would illumine the church, now bringing into vivid relief the row of judges, now the scarlet-coated soldiers, or the golden head of a child and its terror-stricken mother, again playing on and about the pulpit where the impassioned minister, his face ghastly above his black vestments, called unceasingly upon the Lord for succour.

The building was shaken to its foundations.   Still to an heroic degree the people maintained their self-control.

Suddenly there was a more brilliant flash than usual, followed by a loud crash.

When this terrific shock had passed, and each person was beginning to realize dimly that he or she had survived it, the minister's voice was heard singing the fifty-second psalm.

> " Mine enemies daily enterprise
> to swallow me outright ;
> To fight against me many rise,
> O, Thou most high of might."

And this first verse he sang unwaveringly through alone.

With the commencement of the next verse, some few brave, but quavering voices joined him.

> "What things I either did or spake
> they wrest them at their wil,
> And al the councel that they take
> is how to work me il."

But before the third verse ended, all were singing, judges and soldiers, and the sweet voices of the women and the shrill notes of the little children.

> "They al consent themselves to hide
> close watch for me to lay:
> They spie my paths and snares have layd
> to take my life away."

From this time on the storm abated its violence.

When at last the benediction was pronounced, the soldiers and men, in constant dread of attacks by Indians, left the meeting-house before the women and children, thus making sure the safe exit of the latter.

The people, crowding out, beheld the setting sun shining brightly. The odour of the rain and the fresh earth greeted them.   All the trees in the leafy greenness of June quivered with fresh life.

The hail lay white upon the ground as petals new-fallen from cherry trees in bloom.

All nature was refreshed.

Only the mighty oak that had stood near the entrance was split in twain.

And the people,—the goodmen with heads uncovered,—in the mellow light of the departing day, rendered thanks unto God that they had been delivered.

Chapter V

The Coming of the Town Beadle

THE next morning, Goodwife Higgins and Deliverance heard steps coming around the side of the house.

"Who can it be at this hour o' the dawning?" asked the goodwife. "It be but the half-hour past six o' the minute-glass."

"Ye don't hear the tapping o' a stick like as it might be Sir Jonathan, goody," asked Deliverance, listening fearfully. "I like not his ruddy beard and his sharp, greeny-gray eyes."

But as she spoke, the form of the Town Beadle with his Bible and staff of office darkened the doorway.

"Has our cow Clover gotten loose again?" cried Deliverance, remembering the meadow-bars were broken. One of the chief duties connected with the office of Beadle was to arrest stray cows and impose a fine on their owners.

Goodwife Higgins said never a word, only watched the Beadle, her face grown white.

"As much as three weeks ago and over," continued Deliverance, deftly drying a pewter platter, "as I was cutting across the meadow to Abigail Brewster's back door, I saw those broken bars. 'Hiram', says I to the bound boy, 'ye had best mend those bars, or Clover and her calf will get loose and ye get your ears boxed for being a silly loon, and ye ken ye be that, Hiram.' 'I ken,' says he. Hold your dish-cloth over the pan, goody," she added, "it be dripping on the floor."

While she spoke, the Beadle had been turning over the leaves of his Bible. He laid it open face downward on the table, to keep the place, while he carefully adjusted his horn-bowed spectacles on his nose. He cleared his throat.

"Peace be on this household," he announced pompously, "and suffer the evil-doer to be brought out from his dark ways and hiding-place into the public highway where all may be warned by his example." Having delivered himself of these words he raised the Bible and read a stretch therefrom. "Thou shalt not suffer a witch to live, neither wizards that peep and mutter. . . . Regard not them that have familiar spirits, neither seek after them to be defiled by them." He closed the book and removed his spectacles. Then he lifted his staff and tapped Deliverance on the shoulder. "I arrest ye in the name of the law," he cried in a loud voice, "to await your trial for witchery, ye having grievously afflicted your victim, Ebenezer Gibbs."

Deliverance stared horrified at him and, although she opened her mouth to speak, her voice was gone.

Goodwife Higgins dusted off the seat of a stool with her apron and pushed it over to the Beadle. "Sit ye down, goodman, and I will bring ye a glass o' buttermilk. Also I will look for the maid's father who be herb-gathering. As for ye,

Deliverance, go to your room and wait there until this matter be settled." For it had flashed into her mind that if she could get out of the kitchen, while Deliverance went to her room, she could slip around the corner of the house and assist the little maid out of the bedroom window, bidding her conceal herself in the forest.

"Nay," said the Beadle, "I have no time to dilly-dally, as I have five stray cows to return this morning. Yet I will have a glass o' buttermilk to wet my throat. I will watch the witch-maid that she escape not while ye be gone."

The goodwife, the tears rolling down her face, hurried to the spring where the buttermilk was kept.

"I be no so wicked as ye make out," said Deliverance, finding her voice.

"Touch me not," cried the Beadle, jumping back in wondrous spry fashion for so pompous a man, and in his fright overturning the stool, "nay, come not so near. Take your hands off my doublet. Would ye cast a spell on me? Approach no nearer than the length o' this staff."

He turned the stool right side up again
and seated himself to drink the buttermilk the dame brought him.

"Come," he said, rising and giving
back the mug when he had finished, " I
have no time to dally with five cows to be
gotten in."   He drew a stout rope from
his pocket.   "Tie her hands behind her,
gossip," he commanded, " I hanker not for
to touch a witch-maid.   Nay, not so easy,
draw that knot tighter."

Goodwife Higgins, weeping, did as he
bade, then rose and put the little maid's
cap on her.   She slipped some cookies
into Deliverance's work-pocket.

" I be not above cookies myself," remarked the Beadle, quite jovially, and
he helped himself bountifully from the
cooky-jar.

" My father will come after me and
bring me back," murmured Deliverance,
with quivering lips.   "Weep not, dear
goody, for he will explain how it be a
fever sickness that aileth Ebenezer Gibbs,
and no spell o' witchery."

" Step out ahead o' me," commanded

the Beadle, as he put the end of his long staff against her back. "There, keep ye at that distance, and turn not your gaze over your shoulder at me. I ken your sly ways."

Solemnly around the house and out of the gate he marched her, and as the latter swung to behind them, he turned and waved his hand to Goodwife Higgins. "Farewell, gossip," he cried, "I have rid ye o' a witch."

Down the forest road into the town's highway, he marched Deliverance. Many turned to look at them and drew aside with a muttered prayer. The little maid was greatly relieved that they met no naughty boys to hoot and call derisively after her. They were already at their books with the schoolmaster.

At last they reached the jail, in front of which the old jailer sat smoking.

"Bless my soul," he piped, "'tis a pretty maid to be a witch, Beadie. Bide ye at the stoop a bit until I get my bunch o' keys." He hobbled down the corridor inside and disappeared, returning in a few moments jangling a bunch of keys. He stopped half-way down the hall, and unlocking a heavy oaken door, beckoned them to follow.

"Step briskly, Mistress Deliverance," commanded the Beadle, poking her with his staff.

The cell to which she was shown was long and very narrow, and lighted by a small barred window set high in the wall opposite the door. An apple tree growing in Prison Lane thrust its twigs and leaves between the bars. A straw bed was the only furniture. An iron chain, nearly the length of the cell, was coiled in one corner.

"Beshrew me if I like the looks o' that chain," said Deliverance to herself; "I be not at all minded to go in." She wrinkled her nose and sniffed vigorously. "The place has an ill savour. Methinks the straw must be musty," she added out loud.

"Ye shall have fresh to lay on tonight," piped the jailer, "but step in, step in."

"Ay," echoed the Beadle, "step in;" and he poked her again in the back with his stick in a merry fashion quite his own.

Sorely against her will, Deliverance complied. The jailer followed her in and bent over the chain.

"Take care lest she cast a spell on ye to make your bones ache," advised the Beadle, standing safely outside the threshold.

"I be no feared," answered the jailer, whom long experience and familiarity with witches had rendered impervious, "but the lock on this chain ha' rusted an' opens hard."

"Concern yourself not," rejoined the Beadle; "the maid be in no hurry, I wot, and can wait." He laughed hugely at his little joke, and began munching one of the seed-cookies he had brought in his doublet pocket.

Nothing could have exasperated Deliverance more than to see the fat Beadle enjoying the cookies she herself had helped to make, and so she cast such a resentful look at him that he drew quickly back into the corridor beyond her gaze.

"If e'er I set eyes on a witch," he muttered solemnly, "I have this time, for she has a glint in her een that makes my blood run cold."

At the moment her attention was attracted to the Beadle, Deliverance felt a hand clasp her left foot, and in another instant the jailer had snapped the iron ring around her ankle. The other end of the chain was fastened to the wall.

The Beadle's fat face appeared a moment at the side of the door. "A good day to ye, Mistress Deliverance Wentworth," quoth he, "I must away to find my cows. Mistress Deliverance Wentworth, I say, ye had best confess when ye come to trial."

"Ay," retorted Deliverance, "and ye had best be careful lest a witch get ye. Methinks I dreamed one had catched hold on ye by the hair o' your head."

"An' I ha' heerd tell o' evil spirits taking on the form o' a cow," put in the old jailer. He cackled feebly in such malicious fashion that Deliverance shuddered, and felt more fear of this old man with his bent back and toothless jaws than of

the pompous Beadle. To her relief he
did not address her, but left the cell, locking the door after him.

All that day Deliverance waited eagerly,
but her father did not come for her, and
she feared he had been taken ill. She
was confident Goodwife Higgins would
come in his stead, and so sure was she
of this that she slept sweetly, even on
the musty straw the jailer had neglected
to change. But when the second day
passed, and then the third, and the fourth,
until at last the Sabbath came again, and
in all that time no one had come, nor sent
word to her, she grew despondent, fearing
the present and dreading the future under
the terrible strain of hope deferred. The
jailer would have naught to say to her.
At last she ceased to expect any change,
sitting listlessly on her straw bed, finding
one day like another, waiting only for her
trial to come.

Chapter VI

The Woman of Ipswich

THOSE were terrible times in Salem. Day after day the same scenes were enacted. The judges with their cavalcade came in pomp from Ipswich, and rode solemnly down the street to the meeting-house.

The people were as frantic now lest they or their friends be accused of witch-craft, as they had formerly been fearful of suffering from its spells.

That craving for excitement which had actuated so many of the possessed, the opportunity for notoriety long coveted and at last put within reach of the coarsest natures, now began to be regarded in their true light. Moreover, there was a great opening for the wreaking of private hatreds, and many, to quiet their uneasy consciences, persuaded themselves that their enemies were in league with the Devil. But this zeal in pushing the prosecutions was becoming dangerous. For the accused person, confessing, and so granted his liberty, would straightway bring charges against his accusers.

The signs of witchery multiplied in number. Certain spots upon the body were accounted marks of the Devil. Were the victims from age or stupefaction unable to shed tears, it was counted against them. The most ordinary happenings of life, viewed in the light of this superstition, acquired an unnatural significance.

There were those who walked abroad, free, but bearing the burden of a wounded conscience. Many of these found intolerable the loathing and fear which greeted them, and desired that they might have died before they had falsely confessed to a crime of which they were not guilty.

There were rumours, that for any contumacious refusal to answer, the barbarous common English law — peine forte et dure — would be brought in usage.

Two dogs, regarded accomplices in

the horrid crime, were hanged with their owners.

A child not more than four or five years old was also committed as a witch. Her alleged victim showed the print of small teeth in his arm where she had bitten him.

Unbelievers were overwhelmed with evidence. Had not the laws of England for over one hundred and fifty years been in force against witches? Thirty thousand had been executed, and Parliament had lately appointed a witch-finder, who, when he had discovered all the remaining witches in England, so it was said, was to be sent to the colonies. Had not King James written a book against sorcerers and those possessed by the Evil One?

Archbishop Jewell had begged Queen Bess to burn all found guilty of the offence. Above all, the Lord Chief Justice of England had condemned them, and written a book from the Bible upon the subject.

Two weeks from the time she was put in prison, Deliverance was brought to trial.

So high a pitch had the excitement reached, so wrought to a frenzied condition were the villagers, that the authorities had been obliged to take extreme measures, and had forbidden every one except the minister and officers of the law to visit the prisoner.

Thus the little maid had not seen one familiar, loving face during the two weeks previous to her trial.

Aside from her deep trouble and anxiety for fear her father were ill, she grew desperately weary of the long monotonous days. Sometimes she amused herself by writing the alphabet or some Bible verse on the hard earth floor with the point of the pewter spoon that was given her with her porridge. Again she quite forgot her unhappiness, plaiting mats of straw.

Short as her confinement had been, she had lost her pretty colour, and her hands had acquired an unfamiliar whiteness. She had never been released from the iron chain, it being deemed that ordinary fastenings would not hold a witch.

A woman, accused like herself, was

placed in the same cell.   She was brought from Ipswich, owing to the over-crowded condition of the jail in that village.   For two days and nights, Deliverance had wept in terror and abhorrence of her companion.   Yet some small comfort had lain in the fact that the woman was fastened by such a short chain in the further corner that she could not approach the little maid.   Several times she had essayed to talk to Deliverance, but in vain.   The little maid would put her hands over her ears at the first word.

One night, Deliverance had awakened, not with a start as from some terrible dream, but as naturally as if the sunlight, shining on her own little bed at home, had caused her to open her eyes.   So quiet was this awakening that she did not think of her surroundings, but lay looking at the corner of the window visible to her. She saw the moon like pure, bright gold behind the apple-leaves.   After awhile she became conscious of some one near by praying softly.   Then she thought that whoever it was must have been praying a long time, and that she had not observed it; just as one often pays no attention to the murmur of a brook running, hidden in the woods, until, little by little, the sound forces itself upon his ear, and then he hears nothing but the singing of the water. So now she raised herself on her elbow and listened.

In the darkness the cell seemed filled with holy words; then she knew it was the witch praying, and in her prayers she remembered Deliverance. Thereat the little maid's heart was touched.

"Why do ye pray for me?" she asked.

"Because you are persecuted and sorely afflicted," came the answer.

"I ken your voice," said Deliverance; "ye be the witch-woman condemned to die to-morrow. I heard the jailer say so."

"I am condemned by man," answered the woman, "but God shall yet maintain my innocence."

"But ye will be dead," said Deliverance.

"I shall have gone to my Father in heaven," replied the woman, and the darkness hid her worn and glorified face, "but my innocence will be maintained that others may be saved."

"Do ye think that I will be saved?" asked Deliverance.

"Of what do they accuse you?" asked her companion.

"O' witchery," answered Deliverance; and she began to weep.

But the woman, although she might not move near her, comforted her there in the darkness.

"Weep not that men persecute you, dear child. There is another judgment. Dear child, there is another judgment."

For a long time there was silence. Then the woman spoke again. "Dear child," she said, "I have a little son who is a cripple. Should you live and go free, will you see that he suffers not?"

"Where bides he?" asked Deliverance.

"In Ipswich," came the reply. "He was permitted to be with me there in the jail, but when I was brought to Salem, he was taken from me. Will they be kind to him, think you, though he be a witch's child ? "

" I ken not," answered Deliverance.

" Think you they would harden their hearts against one so small and weak, with a crooked back ? " asked the woman.

Deliverance knitted her brows, and strove to think of something comforting she could say, for the woman's words troubled her heart. Suddenly she sat up eagerly, and there was a ring of hope in her sweet, young voice.

" I remember summat which will comfort ye," she cried, " and I doubt not the Lord in His mercy put it into my mind to tell ye." She paused a moment to collect her thoughts.

" I am waiting," said the woman, wistfully ; " dear child, keep me not waiting."

" Listen," said Deliverance, solemnly ; " there be a boy in the village and his name be Submit Hodge. He has a great hump on his back and bandy legs — "

" Thus has my little son," interrupted the woman.

"And he walks on crutches," continued Deliverance.

"My little son is o'er young yet for crutches," said the woman. "I have always carried him in my arms."

"And one day he was going down the street," said Deliverance, resuming her narrative, "when some naughty boys larfed at him and called him jeering names — "

A smothered sob was heard in the other end of the cell.

"Then what should hap," continued Deliverance, "but our reverend judge and godly parson walking arm-in-arm along the street in pious converse, I wot not.   I saw the judge who was about to pass his snuff-box to the parson, forget and put it back in his pocket, and his face go red all at once, for he had spied the naughty boys. He was up with his walking-stick, and I thought it was like to crack the pate o' Thomas Jenkins, who gave over larfing and began to bellow.   But the parson told him to cease his noise ; then he put his arm around Submit Hodge.   Ye ken I happed to hear all this because I was going to a tea-party with my patchwork, and I just dawdled along very slow like, a-smelling at a rose I picked, but with ears wide open.

"And I heard our parson tell the naughty boys that Submit was the Lord's afflicted, and that it was forbid in His Holy Word e'er to treat rudely one who was blind or lame or wanting in gumption or good wits. 'For,' he said, 'they are God's special care. And it be forbid any man to treat them ill.' With that the judge put his hand in his pocket and drew forth a handful of peppermint drops for Submit. And being a high-tempered body, he cracked another boy over his pate with his walking-stick. ''Twill holpen ye to remember your parson's words,' quoth he. And then he and the parson walked on arm-in-arm. When I passed Thomas Jenkins who was bellowing yet, I larfed and snickered audible-like, for I ne'er liked naughty boys. It be a goodly sight to clap eyes on Submit these days, so blithe and gay. Nobody dare tease the lad."

"You comfort me greatly," said the woman; "the Lord's words were in my heart, but in my misery I had nigh forgot them. You have given me peace. Should you be saved, you will not forget my little son. Though you be but a young maid, God may grant you grace to holpen him as is motherless."

" What be his name? " asked Deliverance.

"'Tis Hate-Evil Hobbs," answered the woman; " he lives in Ipswich."

" I will get father to take me there, and I be saved," answered Deliverance, drowsily; " now I will lie down and go to sleep again, for I be more wore-out a-pining and a-weeping o'er my sad condition than e'er I be after a long day's chores at home."

She stretched herself out on the straw and pillowed her head on her arm.

" Good-night, dear child," said the woman. " I will pray that God keep us in the hollow of His hand."

Deliverance, drifting into profound slumber, scarce heard her words. She awoke late. The morning sunshine filled her cell. She was alone. In the corner of the cell, where the woman had lain, were the irons which had fastened her and her straw pallet. Deliverance never saw her again.

Chapter VII

The Trial of Deliverance

AT last one fair June day brought her trial.

Her irons were removed, and she was conducted by the constable with a guard of four soldiers to the meeting-house. In the crowd that parted at the great door to make way for them were many familiar faces, but all were stern and sad. In all eyes she read her accusation. The grim silence of this general condemnation made it terrible ; the whispered comments and the looks cast upon her expressed stern pity mingled with abhorrence.

On the outskirts of the throng she observed a young man of ascetic face and austere bearing, clothed in black velvet, with neck-bands and tabs of fine linen. He wore a flowing white periwig, and was mounted on a magnificent white horse.   In one hand he held the reins, in the other, a Bible.

Upon entering the meeting-house, Deliverance was conducted by the Beadle to a platform and seated upon a stool, above the level of the audience and in plain sight.

In front of the pulpit, the seven judges seated in a row faced the people.   Clothed in all the dignity of their office of crimson velvet gowns and curled white horsehair wigs, they were an imposing array. One judge, however, wore a black skullcap, from beneath which his brown locks, streaked with gray, fell to his shoulders, around a countenance at once benevolent and firm, but which now wore an expression revealing much anguish of mind. This was the great Judge Samuel Sewall, who, in later years, was crushed by sorrow and mortification that at these trials he had been made guilty of shedding innocent blood, so that he rose in his pew in the Old South Church in Boston Town, acknowledging and bewailing his great offence, and asking the prayers of the congregation " that God would not visit the sin of him or of any other upon himself, or any of his, nor upon the land."

In the centre of the group sat Lieutenant-Governor Stoughton, chosen to be chief justice, in that he was a renowned scholar, rather than a great soldier.   Hard and narrow as he was said to be, he yet possessed that stubbornness in carrying out his convictions of what was right, which exercised in a better cause might have won him reputation for wisdom rather than obstinacy.

To the end of his days he insisted that the witch-trials had been meet and proper, and that the only mistakes made had been in checking the prosecutions.   It was currently reported that when the panic subsided, and the reprieve for several convicted prisoners came from Governor Phipps to Salem, he left the bench in anger and went no more into that court.

" For," said he, " we were in a fair way to clear the land of witches.   Who it is that obstructs the cause of justice, I know not. The Lord be merciful unto the country!"

On the left of the prisoner was the jury.

After Deliverance had been duly sworn to tell the truth, she sat quietly, her hands folded in her lap. Now and then she raised her eyes and glanced over the faces upturned to hers. She observed her father not far distant from her. But he held one hand over his eyes and she could not meet his gaze. Beside him sat Goodwife Higgins, weeping.

There was one other who should have been present, her brother Ronald, but he was nowhere to be seen.

The authorities had not deemed it wise to send for him, as it was known he had to a certain extent fallen in with dissenters and free-thinkers in Boston Town, and it was feared that, in the hot blooded impetuosity of youth, he might by some disturbance hinder the trial.

The first witness called to the stand was Goodwife Higgins.

Deliverance, too dazed with trouble to

feel any active grief, watched her with dull eyes.

Weeping, the good dame related the episode of finding the prisoner's bed empty one morning, and the yellow bird on the window-ledge. Groans and hisses greeted her testimony. There was no reason to doubt her word. It was plainly observed that she was suffering, and that she walked over her own heart in telling the truth. It was not simply terror and superstition that actuated Goodwife Higgins, but rather the stern determination bred in the very bone and blood of all Puritans to meet Satan face to face and drive him from the land, even though those dearest and best beloved were sacrificed.

The next witness was the prisoner's father. The heart-broken man had nothing to say which would lead to her conviction. Save the childish naughtiness with which all parents were obliged to contend, the prisoner had been his dear and dutiful daughter, and God would force them to judge her righteously.

" She has bewitched him. She has not even spared her father. See how blind he is to her sinfulness," the whisper passed from mouth to mouth. And hearts hardened still more toward the prisoner.

Master Wentworth was then dismissed. While on the stand he had not glanced at his daughter. Doubtless the sight of her wan little face would have been more than he could have endured.

Sir Jonathan Jamieson was then called upon to give his testimony. As his name was cried by the constable, Deliverance showed the first signs of animation since she had been taken from the jail. Surely, she thought, he who understood better than she the meaning of her words to him, would explain them and save her from hanging. Her eyes brightened, and she watched him intently as he advanced up the aisle. A general stir and greater attention on the part of the people was apparent at his appearance. A chair was placed for him in the witness-box, for he was allowed to sit, being of the gentry. As usual he was clothed in sombre velvet.

He seated himself, took off his hat and laid it on the floor beside his chair. Deliverance then saw that the hair on his head was quite as red as his beard, and that he wore it cropped short, uncovered by a wig. Deliberately, while the judges and people waited, he drew off his leathern gauntlets that he might lay his bare hand upon the Bible when he took the oath.

Deliverance for once forgot her fear of him. She leant forward eagerly. So near was he that she could almost have touched him with her hand.

"Oh, sir," she cried, using strong old Puritan language, "tell the truth and mortify Satan and his members, for he has gotten me in sore straits."

"Hush," said one of the judges, sternly, "let the prisoner keep silent."

"Methinks that I be the only one not allowed to speak," said Deliverance to herself, "which be not right, seeing I be most concerned." And she shook her head, very greatly perplexed and troubled.

Sir Jonathan was then asked to relate what he knew about the prisoner. With much confidence he addressed the court. Deliverance was astonished at the mild accents of his voice which had formerly rung so harshly in her ears.

"I have had but short acquaintance with her," he said, "though I may have passed her often on the street, not observing her in preference to any other maid; but some several weeks ago as I did chance to stop at the town-pump for a draught o' cold water, the day being warm and my throat dry, I paused as is meet and right before drinking to give thanks, when suddenly something moved me to glance up, and I saw the prisoner standing on a block near by, laughing irreverently, which was exceeding ill-mannered."

At this Deliverance's cheeks flushed scarlet, for she knew his complaint was quite just. "I did not mean to laugh," she exclaimed humbly, "but some naughty boys had pinned a placard o' the edge o' your cape, and 'twas a fair comical sight."

At this interruption, the seven judges all frowned upon her so severely that she did not dare say another word.

"Now, while I did not suspicion her at the time," continued Sir Jonathan, "I was moved to think there was a spell cast upon the water, for after drinking I had great pain and needs must strengthen myself with a little rum. Later I met our godly magistrate and chanced to mention the incident. He told me the prisoner's name, and how her vanities and backslidings were a sore torment to her father, and that he knew neither peace nor happiness on her account."

At these words Master Wentworth started to his feet. "I protest against the scandalous words uttered by our magistrate," he cried; "ne'er has my daughter brought me aught save peace and comfort. She has been my sole consolation, since her mother went to God."

He sat down again with his hand over his eyes, while many pitying glances were cast upon him.

"Mind him not," said one of the judges

to Sir Jonathan ; " he is sorely afflicted and weighs not his utterances.   Oh, 'how sharper than a serpent's tooth it is to have a thankless child,' " and he glanced sternly at Deliverance.

At these words, she could no longer contain herself, and covering her face with her hands, she sobbed aloud, remembering all her wilfulness in the past.

" What I have to say," continued Sir Jonathan, " is not much.   But straws show the drift of the current, and little acts the soul's bent.   The night of the same day on which I saw the prisoner standing on the block near the town-pump, I went with a recipe to Master Wentworth's home to have him brew me a concoction of herbs. The recipe I brought from England. Knowing he was very learned in the art of simpling, I took it to him.   I found him in his still-room, working.   Having transacted my business, I seated myself and we lapsed into pleasant converse.   While thus talking, he opened the door, called his daughter from the kitchen, and gave her a small task.   At last, as it drew near the ninth hour when the night-watchman would make his rounds, I rose and said farewell to Master Wentworth, he scarce hearing me, absorbed in his simples. As I was about to pass the prisoner, my heart not being hardened toward her for all her vanities, I paused, and put my hand in my doublet pocket, thinking to pleasure her by giving her a piece of silver, and also to admonish her with a few, well-chosen words. But as my fingers clasped the silver piece, my attention was arrested by the expression of the prisoner's face. So full of malice was it that I recoiled. And at this she uttered a terrible imprecation, the words of which I did not fully understand, but at the instant of her uttering them a most excruciating pain seized upon me. It racked my bones so that I tossed sleepless all that night."

He paused and looked around solemnly over the people. "And since then," he added, " I have not had one hour free from pain and dread."

As Sir Jonathan finished his testimony, he glanced at Deliverance, whose head had sunk on her breast and from whose heart all hope had departed. If he would say naught in explanation, what proof could she give that she was no witch? Her good and loyal word had been given not to betray her meeting with the mysterious stranger.

"Deliverance Wentworth," said Chief Justice Stoughton, "have you aught to say to the charge brought against you by this godly gentleman?"

As she glanced up to reply, she encountered the malevolent glance of Sir Jonathan defying her to speak, and she shook with fear. With an effort she looked away from him to the judges.

"I be innocent o' any witchery," she said in her tremulous, sweet voice. The words of the woman who had been in jail with her returned to her memory: "There is another judgment, dear child." So now the little maid's spirits revived. "I be innocent o' any witchery, your Lordships," she repeated bravely, "and there be another judgment than that which ye shall put upon me."

Strange to say, the sound of her own voice calmed and assured her, much as if the comforting words had been again spoken to her by some one else. Surely, she believed, being innocent, that God would not let her be hanged.

The fourth witness, Bartholomew Stiles, a yeoman, bald and bent nearly double by age, was then cried by the Beadle.

Leaning on his stick he pattered up the aisle, and stumblingly ascended the steps of the platform.

" Ye do me great honour, worships," he cackled, " to call on my poor wit."

" Give him a stool, for he is feeble," said the chief justice; " a stool for the old man, good Beadle."

So a stool was brought and old Bartholomew seated upon it. He looked over the audience and at the row of judges. Then he spied Deliverance. " Ay, there her be, worships, there be the witch." He pointed his trembling finger at her. " Ay, witch, the old man kens ye."

" When did you last see the prisoner?" asked the chief justice.

"There her be, worships," repeated the witness, "there be the witch, wi' a white neck for stretching. Best be an old throat wi' free breath, than a lassie's neck wi' a rope around it."

Deliverance shuddered.

"Methinks no hag o' the Evil One," said she to herself, "be more given o'er to malice than this old fule, Lord forgive me for the calling o' him by that name."

Now the judge in the black silk cap was moved to pity by the prisoner's shudder, and spoke out sharply. "Let the witness keep to his story and answer the questions put to him in due order, or else he shall be put in the stocks."

"Up with your pate, goody," admonished the Beadle, "and speak out that their worships may hear, or into the stocks ye go to sweat in the sun while the boys tickle the soles o' your feet."

The witness wriggled uneasily as having had experience.

"A week ago, or it be twa or three or four past, your worships, the day afore this time, 'twixt noon an' set o' sun, there had been thunder an' crook'd lightning, an' hags rode by i' the wind on branches. All the milk clabbered, if that will holpen ye to 'membrance o' the day, worships."

"Ay, reverend judges," called out a woman's voice from the audience, "sour milk the old silly brought me, four weeks come next Thursday. Good pence took he for his clabbered milk, and I was like to cuff—"

"The ducking-stool awaits scolding wives," interrupted the chief justice, with a menacing look, and the woman subsided.

"That day at set o' sun I was going into toone wi' my buckets o' milk when I spied a bramble rose. 'Blushets,' says I to them, 'ye must be picked;' for I thought to carry them to the toone an' let them gae for summat gude to eat. So I set doone my pails to pull a handful o' the pretty blushets. O' raising my old een, my heart was like to jump out my throat, for there adoon the forest path, 'twixt the green, I saw the naughty maid i' amiable converse wi' Satan."

"Dear Lord," interrupted the little maid, sharply, "he was a very pleasant gentleman."

"Silence!" cried the Beadle, tapping her head with his staff, on the end of which was a pewter-ball.

"As ye ken," continued the old yeoman, "the Devil be most often a black man, but this time he was o' fair colour, attired in most ungodly fashion in a gay velvet dooblet wi' high boots. So ta'en up wi' watching o' the wickedness o' Deliverance Wentworth was I, that I clean forgot myself—"

The speaker, shuddering, paused.

"Lose not precious time," admonished the chief justice, sternly.

"O' a sudden I near died o' fright," moaned the old yeoman.

A tremor as at something supernatural passed over the people.

"Ay," continued the witness, "wi' mine very een, I beheld the prisoner turn an' run towards her hame, whilst the Devil rose an' come doone the path towards me, Bartholomew Stiles!"

"And then?" queried the chief justice, impatiently.

"It was too late to hide, an' I be no spry a' running. Plump o' my marrow-boones I dropped, an' closed my een an' prayed wi' a loud voice. I heard Satan draw near. He stopped aside me. 'Ye old silly,' says he, 'be ye gane daffy?' Ne'er word answered I, but prayed the louder. I heard the vision take a lang draught o' milk from the bucket wi' a smackin' o' his lips. Then did Satan deal me an ungentle kick an' went on doon the path."

"Said he naught further?" asked one of the judges.

"Nae word more, worships," replied the yeoman. "I ha' the caution not to open my een for a lang bit o' time. Then I saw that what milk remained i' the bucket out o' which Satan drank, had turned black, an' I ha' some o' it here to testify to the sinfu' company kept by Deliverance Wentworth."

From his pocket the old yeoman carefully drew a small bottle filled with a black liquid, and, in his shaking hand, extended it to the judge nearest him.

Solemnly the judge took it and drew out the cork.

"It has the smell of milk," he said, "but milk which has clabbered;" and he passed it to his neighbour.

"It has the look of clabbered milk," assented the second judge.

"Beshrew me, but it is clabbered milk," asserted the third judge; "methinks 'twould be wisdom to keep the bottle corked, lest the once good milk, now a malignant fluid, be spilled on one of us and a tiny drop do great evil."

Thus the bottle was passed from one judicial nose to the other, and then given to the Beadle, who set it carefully on the table.

There may be seen to this day in Salem a bottle containing the pins which were drawn from the bodies of those who were victims of witches. But the bottle which stood beside it for over a century was at last thrown away, as it was empty save for a few grains of some powder or dust.

Little did they who flung it away realize that that pinch of grayish dust was the remains of the milk, which Satan, according to Bartholomew Stiles, had bewitched, and which was a large factor in securing the condemnation of Deliverance Wentworth.

The next witness was the minister who had conducted the services on the afternoon of that late memorable Sabbath, when the Devil had sought to destroy the meeting-house during a thunder-storm.

He testified to having seen the prisoner raise her eyes, as she entered the church in disgrace ahead of the tithing-man, and instantly an invisible demon, obeying her summons, tore down that part of the roof whereon her glance rested.

This evidence, further testified to by other witnesses, was in itself sufficient to condemn her.

The little maid heard the minister sadly. In the past he had been kind to her, and was her father's friend, and his young daughter had attended the Dame School with her.

Later, this very minister was driven from the town by his indignant parishioners, who blamed him not that he had shared in the general delusion, but that many of his persecutions had been actuated by personal malice.

And by a formal and public act, the repentant people cancelled their excommunication of one blameless woman who had been his especial victim.

"Deliverance Wentworth," said the chief justice, "the supreme test of witchery will now be put to you. Pray God discover you if you be guilty. Let Ebenezer Gibbs appear."

"Ebenezer Gibbs," cried the Beadle, loudly.

At this there was a great stir and confusion in the rear of the meeting-house.

Deliverance saw the stern faces turn from her, and necks craned to see the next witness. There entered the young man whom she had noticed, mounted on a white horse, at the outskirts of the crowd. A buzz of admiration greeted him, as he advanced slowly up the aisle, with a pomposity unusual in so young a man. His expression was austere. His right hand was spread upon a Bible, which he held against his breast. His hand, large, of a dimpled plumpness, with tapering fingers, was oddly at variance with his handsome face, which was thin, and marked by lines of hard study ; a fiery zeal smouldered beneath the self-contained expression, ready to flame forth at a word. He ascended the platform reserved for the judges, and seated himself. Then he laid the Bible on his knees, and folded his arms across his breast.

A pitiful wailing arose in the back of the house, and the sound of a woman's voice hushing some one.

A man's voice in the audience cried out, " Let the witch be hanged. She be tormenting her victim."

" I be no witch," cried Deliverance, shrilly. " Dear Lord, give them a sign I be no witch."

The Beadle pounded his staff for silence.

" Let Ebenezer Gibbs come into court."

Chapter VIII

The Last Witness

IN answer to these summons, a child came slowly up the aisle, clinging to his mother's skirts. His thin little legs tottered under him; his face was peaked and wan, and he hid it in his mother's dress. When the Beadle sought to lift him, he wept bitterly, and had to be taken by force, and placed upon the platform where the accused was seated. The poor baby gasped for breath. His face grew rigid, his lips purple. His tiny hands, which were like bird's claws, so thin and emaciated were they, clinched, and he fell in convulsions.

An angry murmur from the people was instantly succeeded by the deepest silence.

The magistrates and people breathlessly awaited the result of the coming experiment.

The supreme test in all cases of witchery was to bring the victim into court, when he would generally fall into convulsions, or scream with agony on beholding the accused.

The Beadle and his assistants would then conduct or carry the sufferer to the prisoner, who was bidden by the judge to put forth his hand and touch the flesh of the afflicted one. Instantly the convulsions and supposed diabolical effects would cease, the malignant fluid passing back, like a magnetic current, into the body of the witch.

Tenderly the Beadle lifted the small convulsed form of Ebenezer Gibbs and laid it at the prisoner's feet.

"Deliverance Wentworth," said the chief justice, "you are bidden by the court to touch the body of your victim, that the malignant fluid, with which you have so diabolically afflicted him, may return into your own body. Again I pray God in His justice discover you if you be guilty."

Despite the severity of her rule, the

little assistant teacher of the Dame School
had a most tender heart for her tiny
scholars. She bent now and lifted this
youngest of her pupils into her lap.

"Oh, Ebenezer," she cried, stricken
with remorse, "I no meant to rap your
pate so hard as to make ye go daffy."

Doubtless the familiar voice pierced to
the child's benumbed faculties, for he was
seen to stir in her arms.

"Ebenezer," murmured the little maid,
"do ye no love me, that ye will no open
your eyes and look at me? Why, I be no
witch, Ebenezer. Open your eyes and see.
I will give ye a big sugar-plum and ye will."

The beloved voice touched the estranged
child-heart. Perhaps the poor, stricken
baby believed himself again at his knitting
and primer-lesson at the Dame School.
In the awed silence he was seen to raise
himself in the prisoner's arms and smile.
With an inarticulate, cooing sound, he
stroked her cheek with his little hand.
The little maid spoke in playful chiding.
Suddenly a weak gurgle of laughter smote
the strained hearing of the people.

"Ye see, ye see I be no witch," cried Deliverance, raising her head, "ye see he be no afeared o' me."

But as soon as the words left her lips, she shrank and cowered, for she realized that the test of witchery had succeeded, that she was condemned. From her suddenly limp and helpless arms the Beadle took the child and returned it to its mother. And from that hour it was observed that little Ebenezer Gibbs regained strength.

The prisoner's arms were then bound behind her that she might not touch any one else.

After quiet had been restored, and the excitement at this direct proof of the prisoner's guilt had been quelled, the young minister, who had entered at a late hour of the trial, rose and addressed the jury. He was none other than the famous Cotton Mather, of Boston Town, being then about thirty years old and in the height of his power. He had journeyed thither, he said, especially to be present at this trial, inasmuch as he had heard that some doubters had protested that the prisoner being young and a maiden, it was a cruel deed to bring her to trial, as if it had not been proven unto the people, yea, unto these very doubters, that the Devil, in his serpent cunning, often takes possession of seemingly innocent persons.

"Atheism," he said, tapping his Bible, "is begun in Sadducism, and those that dare not openly say, 'There is no God,' content themselves for a fair step and introduction thereto by denying there are witches. You have seen how this poor child had his grievous torment relieved as soon as the prisoner touched him. Yet you are wrought upon in your weak hearts by her round cheek and tender years, whereas if the prisoner had been an hag, you would have cried out upon her. Have you not been told this present assault of evil spirits is a particular defiance unto you and your ministers? Especially against New England is Satan waging war, because of its greater godliness. For the same reason it has been observed that demons, having

much spitred against God's house, do
seek to demolish churchs during thunder-
storms. Of this you have had terrible
experience in the incident of this prisoner. You know how hundreds of poor
people have been seized with supernatural
torture, many scalded with invisible brimstone, some with pins stuck in them,
which have been withdrawn and placed in
a bottle, that you all may have witness
thereof. Yea, with mine own eyes have
I seen poor children made to fly like
geese, but just their toes touching now
and then upon the ground, sometimes not
once in twenty feet, their arms flapping
like wings ! "

The court-house was very warm this
June morning. Cotton Mather paused
to wipe the perspiration from his brow.
As he returned his kerchief to his pocket
his glance rested momentarily on the
prisoner.

For the first time he realized her youth.
He noted her hair had a golden and innocent shining like the hair of a little
child.

"Surely," he spoke aloud, yet more to himself than to the people, "the Devil does indeed take on at times the appearance of a very angel of light!"

He felt a sudden stirring of sympathy for those weak natures wrought upon by "a round cheek and tender years." The consciousness of this leaning in himself inspired him to greater vehemence.

"The conviction is most earnestly forced upon me that God has made of this especial case a very trial of faith, lest we embrace Satan when he appears to us in goodly disguise, and persecute him only when he puts on the semblance of an old hag or a middle-aged person. Yet, while God has thus far accorded the most exquisite success to our endeavour to defeat these horrid witchcrafts, there is need of much caution lest the Devil outwit us, so that we most miserably convict the innocent and set the guilty free. Now, the prisoner being young, meseemeth she was, perchance, more foolish than wicked. And when I reflect that men of much strength and hearty women have confessed that the

Black man did tender a book unto them,
soliciting them to enter into a league with
his Master, and when they refused this
abominable spectre, did summon his demons to torture these poor people, until
by reason of their weak flesh, but against
their real desires, they signed themselves
to be the servants of the Devil forever,
—and, I repeat, that when I reflect on
this, that they who were hearty and of
mature age could not withstand the torture of being twisted and pricked and
pulled, and scalded with burning brimstone, how much less could a weak, tender
maid resist their evil assaults?   And I
trust that my poor prayers for her salvation will not be refused, but that she will
confess and save her soul."

He turned his earnest glance upon Deliverance and, perceiving she was in great
fear, he spoke to her gently, bidding her
cast off all dread of the Devil, abiding
rather in the love of God, and thus strong
in the armour of light, make her confession.

But the little maid was too stupefied by

terror to gather much intelligent meaning from his words, and she stared helplessly at him as if stricken dumb.

At her continued, and to him, stubborn, silence, his patience vanished.

"Then are you indeed obstinate and of hard heart, and the Lord has cast you off," he cried. He turned to the judges with an impassioned gesture. "What better proof could you have that the Devil would indeed beguile the court itself by a fair outward show? Behold a very Sadducee! See in what dire need we stand to permit no false compassion to move us, lest by not proceeding with unwavering justice in this witchery business we work against the very cause of Christ. Still, while I would thus caution you not to let one witch go free, meseemeth it is yet worth while to consider other punishment than by halter or burning. I have lately been impressed by a Vision from the Invisible World, that it would be pleasing to the Lord to have the lesser criminals punished in a mortifying public fashion until they renounce the Devil. I am apt to think there is some substantial merit in this peculiar recommendation."

A ray of hope was in these last words for the prisoner.

Deliverance raised her head eagerly. A lesser punishment! Then she would not be hanged. Oh, what a blessed salvation that she would be placed only in the stocks, or made to stand in a public place until she should confess! And it flashed through her mind that she could delay her confession from day to day until the Cavalier should return.

Cotton Mather caught her sudden changed expression.

The wan little face with its wide, uplifted eyes and half parted lips acquired a fearful significance. That transfiguring illumination of hope upon her face was to him the phosphorescent playing of diabolical lights.

His compassion vanished. He now saw her only as a subtle instrument of the Devil's to defeat the ministers and the Church. He shuddered at the train of miserable consequences to which his pity might have opened the door, had not the mercy of God showed him his error in time.

"But when you have catched a witch of more than ordinary devilment," he cried, striking the palm of one hand with his clinched fist, "and who, by a fair and most subtle showing, would betray the cause of Christ to her Master, let no weak pity unnerve you, but have at her and hang her, lest but one such witch left in the land acquire power to wreak untold evil and undo all we have done."

Still once again did his deeply concerned gaze seek the prisoner's face, hoping to behold therein some sign of softening.

Beholding it not he sighed heavily. He would willingly have given his life to save her soul to the good of God and to the glory of his own self-immolation.

"I become more and more convinced that my failure to bring this miserable maid to confession, and indeed the whole assault of the Evil Angels upon the country," he continued, using those words which have been generally accepted as a revelation of his marvellous credulity and self-righteousness, "were intended by Hell as a particular defiance unto my poor endeavours to bring the souls of men unto heaven. Yet will I wage personal war with Satan to drive him from the land."

He raised his eyes, a light of exaltation sweeping over his face.

"And in God's own appointed time," he cried in a voice that quivered with emotion, "His Peace will again descend upon this fair and gracious land, and we shall be at rest from persecution."

Whatever of overweening vanity his words expressed, none present seeing his enraptured face might have judged him harshly.

No infatuated self-complacency alone prompted his words, but rather his earnest conviction that he was indeed the instrument of God, and believed himself by reason of his long fastings and prayer, more than any person he knew, in direct communion with the invisible world.

And if his vanity and self-sufficiency

held many from loving him, there were few who did not involuntarily do him honour.

Having finished he sat down, laid his Bible on his knee, and folded his arms across his breast as heretofore. None, looking at him then as he sat facing the people, his chest puffed out with incomparable pride, young, with every sign of piety, withal a famous scholar, and possessed of exceptional personal comeliness, saw how the shadow of the future already touched him, when for his honest zeal in persecuting witches he should be an object of insult and ridicule in Boston Town, people naming their negroes Cotton Mather after him.

During his speech, Deliverance had at first listened eagerly, but, as he continued, her head sank on her breast and hope vanished. Dimly, as in a dream, she heard the judges' voices, the whispering of the people. At last, as a voice speaking a great distance off, she heard her name spoken.

" Deliverance Wentworth," said Chief

Justice Stoughton, "you are acquaint with the law. If any man or woman be a witch and hath a familiar spirit, or hath consulted with one, he or she shall be put to death. You have by full and fair trial been proven a witch and found guilty in the extreme. Yet the court will shew mercy unto you, if you will heartily, and with a contrite heart, confess that you sinned through weakness, and repent that you did transfer allegiance from God to the Devil."

"I be no witch," cried Deliverance, huskily, "I be no witch. There be another judgment."

The tears dropped from her eyes into her lap and the sweat rolled down her face. But she could not wipe them away, her arms being bound behind her.

The judge nearest her, he who wore his natural hair and the black cap, was moved to compassion. He leant forward, and with his kerchief wiped the tears and sweat from her face.

"You poor and pitiful child," he said, "estranged from God by reason of your

great sin, confess, confess, while there is
yet time, lest you be hanged in sin and
your soul condemned to eternal burning."

Deliverance comprehended but the
merciful act and not the exhortation.
She looked at him with the terror and
entreaty of a last appeal in her eyes, but
was powerless to speak.

Chapter IX

In which Abigail sees Deliverance

THUS because she would not confess to the crime of which she had been proven guilty in the eyes of the law, she was sentenced to be hanged within five days, on Saturday, not later than the tenth nor earlier than the eighth hour. Also, owing to the fact of the confusion and almost ungovernable excitement among the people, it was forbidden any one to visit her, excepting of course the officers of the law, or the ministers to exhort her to confession.

At noon the court adjourned.

First, the judges in their velvet gowns went out of the meeting-house. With the chief justice walked Cotton Mather, conversing learnedly.

Following their departure, two soldiers entered and bade Deliverance rise and go out with them.   So, amidst a great silence, she passed down the aisle.

Then the people were allowed to leave. Some of them must needs follow the judges, riding in stately grandeur down the street to the tavern for dinner.   But the greater part of them followed the prisoner's cart to the very door of the jail.

As Deliverance stepped from the cart, she saw a familiar figure near by.   It was that of Goodwife Higgins.

"Deliverance, oh, Deliverance," cried the poor woman, "speak to me, my bairn!"

But Deliverance looked at her with woebegone eyes, answering never a word.

The goodwife, regardless of the angry warnings of the guard to stand back, pushed her way to her foster-child's side.   Deliverance was as one stricken dumb.   Only she raised her face, and the goodwife bent and kissed the little maid's parched lips.

A soldier wrested them violently apart. "Are ye gone daft, gossip," he cried harshly, "that ye would buss a witch?"

Of the many that had packed the meeting-house to the full that morning, but one person now remained in it. This was Master Wentworth, the simpler, honoured for his pure and blameless life as well as for his great skill. All that summer noontide he knelt and prayed, unmindful of the heat, the buzzing flies, the garish light streaming through the window. He, knowing that the hearts of men were hardened to his cause, had carried his grief to a higher Tribunal.

When the jailer had turned the key in the door and locked her in, a certain peace came to Deliverance.

The abhorred prison-cell now seemed sweet to her. No longer was it a prison, but a refuge from the stern faces, the judges, and the young minister. Never had the lavender-scented sheets of her little hooded bed at home seemed half so sweet as did now the pile of straw in the corner. Once more the chain was fastened around her ankle. But the clanking of this chain was music to her compared to the voices that had condemned her.

The sunlight came in the window with

a green and golden glory through the leaves of the gnarled old apple tree.

Drearily the long afternoon wore away. Deliverance wondered why she did not cry, but she seemed to have no tears left, and she felt no pain. So she began to believe her heart had indeed grown numb, much as her fingers did in cold weather. She longed to know if the stranger she had met in the forest had yet arrived from Boston Town. However, she felt that if he had he would have found her before this. Something entirely unforeseen must have detained him. Had he not said he would return in state in a few days? Toward sunset she heard a rustling in the leaves of the apple tree and the snapping of twigs as if a strong wind had suddenly risen. She looked up at the window. Something was moving in the tree. After a breathless moment, she caught a glimpse of the sad-coloured petticoat of Abigail Brewster. Her heart throbbed with joy. The leaves at the window were parted by two small, sunbrowned hands, and then against the bars was pressed a sober face, albeit as round and rosy as an apple, and two reproachful brown eyes gazed down upon her.

"Deliverance," asked the newcomer, "might ye be a witch and ne'er telled me a word on it?"

Hope came back with a glad rush to Deliverance and lit her eyes with joy, and touched her cheeks with colour. For several moments she could not speak. Then the tears streamed from her eyes, and she put forth her arms, crying, "Oh, Abigail, I be fair glad to see ye!   I be fair glad to see ye."

"I thought ye would have telled me on it," repeated Abigail.

"Ye be right," answered the little maid, solemnly, "I be no witch.   I speak true words, Abigail.   I ken not how to be a witch and I would."

"I calculate ye were none," answered the other, "for ye were ne'er o'er quick to be wicked save in an idle fashion.   I calculate ye would ne'er meddle with witches. Ye were gone so daffy o'er the adorning o' your sinful person that ye had thought for nothing else in your frowardness and vanity." Severe though the words were, the speaker's voice trembled and suddenly broke into sobs. "Oh, Deliverance, Deliverance, I ken not what I shall do and ye be hanged! I tell ye a wicked witch has done this, and hanged her evil deeds on ye to escape her righteous punishment."

"Ye silly one, hush your soughing," whispered Deliverance, sharply, "or the jailer will hear ye and send ye away." She glanced toward the door to assure herself that it was closed, then whispered, "The Lord has put into my mind a plan by which ye can free me, and ye be so minded."

"I ken not how to refrain from soughing when I think o' ye hanging from the gallows, swinging back and forth, back and forth," wept Abigail.

Deliverance shuddered. "Ye were ne'er too pleasant-mouthed," she retorted with spirit, despite the terrible picture drawn for her; "but ye be grown fair evil and full o' malice to mind me o' such an awful thing."   She pointed frantically to the door.   "Hush your soughing, ye silly one.   Methinks I hear the jailer."

"Ye look no reconciled to God, Deliverance," protested Abigail, meekly, wiping her eyes on the edge of her linsey-woolsey petticoat.

"Now hark ye, Abigail," said Deliverance, "and I will tell ye an o'er-strange tale.   But ye must swear to me that ye will breathe no word o' it.   I be on a service for his Majesty, the King, the likes ye wot not of.   And now no more of this lest I betray a secret I be bound in all loyalty to keep.   But in proof o' my words, that it be no idle tale, ye can go to-morrow morning to the old oak tree with the secret hollow, and run your arm into the hole and feel around until you touch summat hard and small, wrapped in a bit o' silk.   Ye will see the package contains a string o' gold beads which ye can look at and try on; for it is great consolation to feel ye have on good gold beads.   Watch out, meantime, that no witch spy ye.   Then wrap them up, and put them back, and run fast away so ye be no tempted to fall into the sin o' envy by lingering, for ye be o'er much given to hankering for worldly things, Abigail."

"I ken, I ken," cried Abigail, breaking into sobs, "that I be no so spiritual minded as I ought to be. But, oh, Deliverance, my unchastened heart be all so full o' woe and care to think o' ye in prison, that I cannot sleep o' nights for weeping, and I continually read the Script-ures comforting against death. But I can find no comfort for thinking on the good times we have had together, and so I fear I be a great reproach unto God."

"Hush, hush!" cried Deliverance, "I hear some one coming."

There was a moment of fearful listening. Then the approaching footsteps passed the door and went on down the corri-dor.

"Now, I have thought out a plan which be summat like this," continued Deliverance. "Ye must take a letter to Boston Town for me. If ye start early and don't dawdle by the way, ye will

reach there by set o' sun.   Still, if ye
should not arrive until dusk, ye could ask
the night watchman the way.   And I
should advise ye to put on no airs as
being acquaint with the town, but to inquire humbly o' him the way to Harvard
College.   I doubt not he will be pleased
to tell ye civilly it be up the street a little
ways, like as the boys' school be here.
So ye must walk on, and when ye have
reached it, raise the knocker and rap, and
go in.   There ye will see one young man,
much more learned and good to look at
than his fellows, and he will be my dear
and only brother, Ronald.   After ye
have asked the goodly schoolmaster
permission, ye must go up and pluck
hold o' Ronald by his doublet sleeve, and
draw him down to whisper in his ear o'
my sore plight.   Now, I think ye will
find all this to be just as I say, though I
have ne'er been in Boston Town.   Ronald
will go with ye to search for the fine
gentleman I met in the forest.   Then,
when he has found him, they will both
come and take me out o' jail.   Bring me

some paper and an ink-horn and quill, so I can write the letter to-morrow."

" I will come as soon as I can," said Abigail. " I would have come before this to-day, but some horrid boys were playing ball in Prison Lane, and I was afeared lest they should see me climb the tree, and suspicion summat."

For the next hour, the two little maids planned a course of action which they fondly hoped would free Deliverance.

" Happen like ye have seen my father, lately?" asked Deliverance, very wistfully, just before they said good-by.

" So sad he looks," answered Abigail; " shall I whisper to him that I have talked with ye?"

" Nay," said Deliverance, " wait until ye have returned from Boston Town with good news. Speaking o' news, did ye hear whether or no a woman by the name o' Hobbs was hanged last week?"

" That I did," replied Abigail. " Father taked me to the hanging. A most awful old witch was she, for sure, with bones like to come through her skin. A judgment o' God's it was come upon her."

"Oh, Abigail," wailed Deliverance, "she was no witch. She said many holy words for me and prayed God forgive her judges. She was in this cell with me."

"They shut a witch in with ye!" cried Abigail, aghast; "she might have cast a spell on ye."

"She cast no spell on me," answered Deliverance, sadly. "Go now, lest ye be missed, and forget not to bring me the paper, quill, and ink-horn."

Ere Abigail could reply there were heavy footsteps in the corridor. They paused at the door.

"Get ye gone quick, Abigail," whispered Deliverance, "some one be coming in. Oh, make haste!" With wildly beating heart she lay down on the straw and shut her eyes.

She heard the jailer speaking to some one as he unlocked the door. Unable to control her curiosity as to the identity of this second person, she opened her eyes, but closed them again spasmodically.

Of the two persons standing on the threshold, one was the bent old jailer: the other — she quivered with dread. Through her shut lids she seemed to see the familiar figure in its cape of sable velvet, the red beard, the long nose beneath the steeple-crowned hat.

The jailer had begun to have doubts regarding the justice of the law, and his heart was in a strange ferment of dissatisfaction, for he thought the Devil had taken upon himself the names and forms of people doubtless innocent.

Moreover, the witch looked so like his own little granddaughter that he grumbled at permitting Sir Jonathan to disturb her.

"Let the poor child sleep," he said, "child o' the Devil though she be. Witch or no, I say, let her sleep if she can after such a day as this. Be no disturbing her, Sir Jonathan. Ye can come again i' the morning, sith ye have gotten permission o' the magistrate."

"Very well, goodman, very well," answered Sir Jonathan, "you are doubtless right. I bethink myself that she would be in no mood for amiable converse. But I will come to-morrow, bright and early." He clapped the jailer on the shoulder and laughed sardonically. " Ha, ha, goodman, 'tis the early bird that catches the worm. Best close a witch's mouth, I say, lest she fly away to bear tales."

Chapter X

A Little Life sweetly Lived

DELIVERANCE awakened happily the next morning for she had been dreaming of home, but as she glanced around her, her smile vanished. Nevertheless, her heart was lighter than it had been for many days. Moreover, she was refreshed by slumber and was surprised to find she enjoyed her breakfast.

She no longer dreaded the anticipated visit of Sir Jonathan. He seemed only an evil dream which had passed with the night. Yet when she heard the tap of his awful stick in the corridor, and his voice at the door, she had no doubt he was a terrible reality. So great was her fear that she could not raise her voice to greet him when he entered, although, remembering her manners, she rose and, despite the clanking chain, courtesied.

He came in pompously, flinging the flaps of his cape back, revealing his belted doublet and the sword at his side.

"'Tis o'er close and warm in here," he said; "methinks you have forgotten a seat for me, goodman."

"Ha' patience, ha' patience," muttered the old jailer, "I be no so young and spry as ye, your lordship." Grumbling, he left the cell.

While Sir Jonathan waited, he leant against the door-casing, swinging his cane in time to a song he hummed, paying no attention to the little maid. The jailer brought him a three-legged stool. He seated himself opposite the little maid, saying naught until the old man had closed the door and turned the key.

Deliverance dared not raise her eyes.

Sir Jonathan observed her sharply from underneath his steeple-hat, his hands clasped on the top of his walking-stick.

This little witch appeared harmless enough, with the fringe of yellow hair cut straight across her round forehead. The rosy mouth was tightly compressed; from beneath the blue-veined lids, two tears forced themselves and hung on her eyelashes.

"There is no need to be afeared of me," said he. "I come only from a godly desire to investigate how you became a witch, for I am thinking of writing a learned book on the evil art of witchery, which shall serve as a warning to meddlers. Also I seek to lead you to confess, ere it be too late and you descend into the brimstone pit."

Deliverance had heard such words before and known them to be for her soul's good. But her heart was hardened toward her present visitor, and his words made no more impression upon her than water dropping on stone. She looked up bravely.

"Good sir," she said staunchly, "the King sends for his black powder."

Sir Jonathan's face grew white and he stared at her long. He opened his mouth to reply, but his dry lips closed without a sound. He jumped up, overturning the stool, and paced up and down the cell.

"You witch!" he cried: "for I 'gin to think you are a witch and a limb of Satan."

Deliverance prayed aloud, for she feared he would strike her with his walking-stick.

Sir Jonathan paused and listened with amazement. At last he laughed abruptly. "Are you indeed a witch, or are you gone daft and silly that you pray?"

"I be no witch," replied the little maid with dignity, "and it be no daffy nor silly to pray. And if it seemeth so to ye, ye be a most ungodly man and the burning pit awaits ye."

Sir Jonathan turned up the stool and sat down again.

"Mistress Deliverance Wentworth," quoth he, wagging his red beard at her, "children were not so illy brought up in my young days. They were reared in righteous fear of their elders and betters. But I have important business with you and no time to talk of froward children. Now, you will please tell me who taught you the lesson you repeat so well."

Deliverance answered never a word.

Sir Jonathan regarded her anxiously. " I could go to the magistrate and have you forced to speak," he said slowly, after awhile, " but 'tis a very private matter." Suddenly a light broke over his countenance. " Ha, ha, my fine bird," he cried, " I have caught you now! You saw the parchment with the royal seal I left with your father."

" Good sir," she answered wonderingly, " I wot not what ye mean."

" You have been well taught," he said, frowning.

" Ay, good sir," she replied sincerely, " I have been most excellently taught."

He puzzled long, shaking his head anon, gazing steadily at the ground.

" Mistress," said he at last, looking up eagerly, " I had no thought of it before, but the man in the forest — who might he be? Ay, that is the question. Who was he? In velvet, with slashed sleeves, the old yeoman said. Come, come," tapping the floor with his walking-stick, " who was this fine gentleman? "

Deliverance perceived he was greatly

perturbed, as people are who stumble inadvertently upon their suspicions of the worst.

"I cannot get through my head," said he, "who this fine gentleman might be. Come, tell me of what sort was this fine Cavalier."

Deliverance made no reply.

"I am sore perplexed," muttered Sir Jonathan; "this business savours ill. I fear I wot not what. Alack! ill luck has pursued me since I left England. Closer than a shadow, it has crept at my heels, ever ready to have at my throat."

So real was his distress that Deliverance was moved to pity. For the moment she forgot his persecution. "I be right sorry for ye," said she.

Now as Sir Jonathan heard the sympathy in the sweet voice, a crafty look came into his eyes, and his lids dropped for fear the little maid might perceive thereby the thought that crossed his mind. He rested his elbow on his knee, bowed his head on his hand, and sighed heavily.

"Could you but know how persecuted

a man I am, mistress," said he, "you would feel grief for my poor cause. Alackaday, alackaday! that I should have such an enemy."

"Who might your enemy be, good sir?" asked the little maid.

"You would not know him," he answered. "In England he dwells,—a man of portly presence, with a dash, a swagger, a twirl of his sword. A man given o'er to dress."

Now, in thinking he could surprise Deliverance into admitting that the fine gentleman she had met that eventful day in the forest was a man of such description, he was mistaken, for the little maid had been taught to keep a close mouth.

"Perchance, I had best tell you my sad tale," continued Sir Jonathan. "I was obliged to flee England, lest mine enemy poison me. Spite of his open air and swagger, he was a snake in the grass, forever ready to strike at my heel, to sting me covertly in darkness. An honest man knows no defence against such a villain. Why look you so at me? I harbour no malice against you."

"But why, good sir," said she, "and ye bore me no malice, did ye tell the reverend judges that I had muttered an imprecation, and cast a spell on ye?"

"How did you know the words you spoke, words which filled me with bitterness and pain, unless you have a familiar spirit?" he asked.

"No familiar spirit have I," answered Deliverance, pitifully. "I be no witch to mutter unco words."

"I know not, I know not," said Sir Jonathan, shrugging his shoulders; "but I shall believe you a witch and you be unable to explain those words."

"Oh, lack-a-mercy-me!" said Deliverance. "Oh, lack-a-mercy-me, whatever shall I do!" And she lifted her petticoat, and wiped her eyes and sighed most drearily.

Sir Jonathan sighed also in a still more dreary fashion.

"This be fair awful," said Deliverance. "I ken not which to believe, ye or the gentleman in the forest."

"What said he?" asked Sir Jonathan, eagerly.

"Nay, good sir," protested Deliverance, "I must have time to think." Even as she spoke, she recalled the stranger's smile, the love-light in his eyes as he showed her the miniature of his sweetest daughter. All doubt that he had deceived her was swallowed up in a wave of keenest conviction that only an honest gentleman could so sincerely love his daughter,—even as her father loved her. And all the former distrust and resentment she had entertained toward Sir Jonathan came back with renewed force.

"I will not tell ye," she said. "Have I not given my good and loyal word? Nay, good sir, I will not tell ye."

"There are ways to make stubborn tongues speak," he threatened.

Deliverance pursed up her mouth obstinately, and looked away from him.

Sir Jonathan pondered long.

"There are ways," he muttered. "Nay, I would not be ungentle. We'll strike a goodly bargain. Come now, my pretty mistress, tell me the secret the stranger telled you. It has brought you naught but grief. I promise, and you do, that you shall not be hanged. How like you that?"

At these words Deliverance paled. "How could ye keep me from being hanged, good sir?" she faltered, and hung her head. She did not meet his glance for very shame of the thought which made parleying with him possible, — the desire to save herself.

"Ay, trust me," he replied. "I will be true to my bargain and you tell me the truth. I am a person of importance, learning, and have mickle gold. This I tell with no false assumption of modesty," he added pompously. "I will tell the magistrates that I have discovered the witch who hanged her evil deeds on you, that the law has laid hold of the wrong person. Then will I demand that you have a new trial."

Deliverance began to sob, for at his words all her terror of being hanged returned. Suppose Abigail should fail, — she grew faint at the thought.

Was it not better to tell the secret and return to her poor father, to Ronald, and to Goodwife Higgins? So she wept bitterly for shame at the temptation which assailed her, and for terror lest she should be hanged.

"Good sir!" she cried piteously, "I pray ye tempt me not to be false to my word. I pray ye, leave me."

Sir Jonathan rose. A fleeting smile of triumph appeared on his face. "Think well of my words, mistress," said he; "to-morrow at this time I will come for my answer." He knocked on the door with his walking-stick for the jailer to come and let him out. While he waited, he hummed lightly an Old World air, and brushed off some straws which clung to his velvet clothes.

Deliverance, still weeping, hid her face in her hands, deeply shamed. For she feared what her answer would be on the morrow.

The jailer returned from showing Sir Jonathan out. He picked up the stool to take it away, yet hesitated to go.

"I ha' brought ye a few goodies," he said, and dropped the sweetmeats in her lap.

"I thank ye," said Deliverance, humbly, "but I have no stomach for them."

Still the old man lingered. "Mayhaps ye confessed to his lordship?"

"I be no witch," said Deliverance.

The old man nodded. "Ay, it be what they all say. It be awful times. I ha' lived a long life, mistress, but I ne'er thought to see such sights." He tiptoed to the threshold, and looked up and down the corridor to assure himself none were near to hear. "I ha' my doubts," he continued, returning to the little maid, "I ha' my doubts. I wot not there ha' been those that ha' been hanged, innocent as the new-born babe. Who kens who will next be cried upon as a witch? As I sit a-sunning in the doorway, smoking my pipe, the whilst I nod i' greeting to the passers-by, I says to myself, 'Be not proud because ye be young, or rich, or a scholar. Ye may yet be taked up for a witch, an' the old jailer put i' authority o'er ye.'"   He lifted the stool again.   "I ha' my doubts," he muttered, going out and locking the door.

Late in the afternoon Abigail came again.

"Deliverance," she said, "be ye there?" She could not see Deliverance, who lay on her straw bed beneath the window.

A meek voice from the darkness below replied, "I be here wrestling with Satan." Deliverance rose as she spoke.   "Oh, Abigail," she said, meeting her friend's glance, "I be sore bruised, buffeting with Satan.   I fear God has not pardoned my sins.   I be sore tempted.   Sir Jonathan was here to-day."

"Bah, the Old Ruddy-Beard," sniffed Abigail, "with his stick forever tapping and his sharp nose poking into everybody's business!   I suspicion he be a witch. Where gets he his mickle gold?"

"He be a wicked man," answered Deliverance, "and now I do perceive he be sent o' the Lord to test my strength. But have ye heard yet o' the fine gentleman I telled ye o' yesterday?"

"Nay," replied Abigail.

"Then summat unforeseen has held him in Boston Town, for the more I think o' his goodly countenance, the more convinced I be o' his goodly heart, though he be high-stomached and given o'er to dress, which ye ken be not the way to heaven," continued Deliverance.   "Did ye bring the paper?"

"I brought my diary," answered Abigail, "and ye can tear out as many pages as ye need, but no more, and I also brought ye your knitting that ye might have summat to do."

She lowered by a string the little diary, the tiny ink-horn and quill, and a half-finished stocking, the needles thrust through the ball of yarn.

In cautious whispers, with eyes anxiously fastened on the door lest it open, the two little maids planned every detail of the course of action they had decided to follow.

But after Abigail had said good-night, Deliverance sat motionless a long time. All knowledge of the village came to her only in the sounds that floated through the window.   She heard the jingle of bells and a mild lowing, and knew it was milking-time and that the cows were being driven home through Prison Lane. She wondered if Hiram had yet mended the meadow bars. Later she heard the boys playing ball in the lane, and she seemed to see the greensward tracked by cow-paths and dotted by golden buttercups. At last the joyous shoutings of the boys ceased and gave way to the sound of drumming. She could see the town-drummer walking back and forth on the platform above the meeting-house door, calling the people to worship.

Suddenly she thought of her father. She put forth her arms, reaching in vain embrace. " Oh, my dear father," she cried, and her voice broke with longing, " oh, my dear father, I be minded o' ye grieving for me all so lonesome in the still-room! Alas, who will pluck ye June roses for the beauty waters ? "

Sad though her thoughts were that she could not see him, yet these very thoughts of him at last brought her peace.

She knew that Sir Jonathan's proposal

to procure a new trial for her had found favour in her heart, and she feared what her answer would be on the morrow. Underneath her tears and prayers, underneath her gladness and relief to see Abigail and the plans they had devised, was the shamed determination to reveal the secret rather than be hanged. She would hold out to the last moment, then — if Abigail were able to accomplish nothing — the little maid's cheeks burned in the darkness, burned with such shame at her guilty resolve that she put her hands over them.

In the darkness she saw forming a shadowy picture of the dearest face in the world to her, her father's long thin face, with its kindly mouth and mild blue eyes. All her life Deliverance believed that, in some mysterious way, her father came to her in prison that night. However it was, she thought that he asked her no question, but seemed to look down into her heart and see all her shame and weakness.

She shrank from his gaze, putting her hands over her breast to hide her heart away from him.   Was it not better, she urged, she should commit just one small sin, and return to him and Ronald, and live a long life so good that it would atone for the wrong-doing?

But he answered that a little life sweetly lived was longer in God's sight than a life of many years stained by sin.

She asked him if it were not a great pain to be hanged when one was innocent, and he admonished her that it was a greater pain to lose one's loyal word and betray one's King who was next to God in authority.

All at once he faded away in a bright light.   Deliverance opened her eyes and found that the long night had passed, that the morning had come, and that she must have been dreaming.   She lay silent for a long time before rising.   All the shame of yesterday had gone from her heart, which was washed clean and filled with peace. She whispered very softly the words of her dream, A little life sweetly lived.

Her hour of temptation was passed.

Thus Deliverance knew God had pardoned her sins.

Chapter XI

Abigail goes to Boston Town

THAT same morning, while it was still in the cool of the day and the sun cast long shadows across the dew-wet grass, Abigail was making her way along the forest path which led to Deliverance's home. In a pail she carried ginger-cookies her mother had sent in exchange for some of Goodwife Higgins' famous cheeseballs.

Since such woeful misfortune had befallen its little mistress, the farmhouse seemed to have acquired a sorrowful aspect. The gate swung open dismally, and weeds had sprung up boldly in the garden. Abigail went round to the kitchen.

It was empty. The floor had been freshly sprinkled with sand; the milkpans were scoured and shining in the sun; a black pot, filled with water, swung over the fire, and Deliverance's kitten slumbered on the hearthstone.

Abigail placed the pail of cookies on the table and seated herself to await Goodwife Higgins' return. Soon the goodwife entered, bearing a big golden pumpkin from the storehouse.

"I be glad to see ye, Abigail, if a sorrowful heart kens aught o' gladness," she said, putting down the pumpkin. "Ye look well and prosperous. I wonder if my little Deliverance has sufficient to eat and warm clothing o' night. I have reared her tenderly, only to strike her a blow when most she needed me. I carry a false and heavy heart." She sat down and, flinging her apron over her head, sobbed aloud.

Abigail longed to tell the poor dame she had seen Deliverance, but dared not.

After a little, the goodwife drew her apron from her head and wiped her eyes with a corner of it. "Hark ye, Abigail, the Lord has punished me, that I took it upon myself to be a judge o' witches. Ye recall how I telled the reverend judges I had seen a yellow bird. I saw that bird again at rise o' sun this morn."

Abigail shivered, although the fire was warm, and glanced around apprehensively. "It was the witch," she cried, "what hanged her evil deeds on Deliverance."

"It was no witch," cried the goodwife. "I would it had been a witch."

Abigail edged off her stool. "I must be going," she said; "methinks I hear a witch scratching on the floor."

But her companion pushed her back. "Sit ye down. I have summat to tell ye. The hand o' the Lord be in it, and laid in judgment on me. Betimes this morn, led o' the Lord, I went to Deliverance's room. There on the sill was the yellow bird. My heart was so full o' sadness, there was no room for fear. 'Gin ye be a witch, ye yellow bird,' said I, 'ye will have hanged a maid that knew not sin.' At this the bird flew off and lighted in the red oak tree o' the edge o' the clearing. I put my Bible in my pocket and hurried out after it. As I neared the red oak, I shuddered, for I thought to find the bird changed into an hag with viper eyes. But naught was to be seen. I looked up into the branches. I cried, 'Ye shall not escape me, ye limb o' Satan,' and with that I clomb the tree. It was a triumph o' the flesh at my years, and proof that the Lord was holpen me. As I stood on the lower branches, I spied a nest and four eggs. I heard a peep, and saw the mother-bird had fluttered off a little way. At her call came the yellow bird, her mate, and flew in my face. Then I was minded these very birds nested there last spring. I suspicioned all. My little Deliverance had scattered crumbs on the window-ledge for the birds."

"Did ye look for to see?" asked Abigail.

The goodwife nodded sadly. "Ay, I found many in the cracks. I be going to see the magistrate and confess my grievous mistake. Bide ye here, Abigail, whilst I be gone, as Master Wentworth has gone herb-gathering. I will stop by and leave the cream cheeses at your mother's."

Left alone, Abigail tied on an apron and went briskly to work at the task the dame

M

had given her. She cut the best part of the pumpkin into dice an inch square, in order to make a side dish to accompany meat. When well made it was almost as good as apple sauce. Having cut the pumpkin up, she put it into a pot, and poured over it a cup of cider-vinegar. Then she swung the pot on the lugpole and stirred the fire. She sighed with relief when the task was finished. At last she was free to attend to Deliverance's errand. Was ever anything so fortunate as the goodwife's mission to the village?

She opened the still-room door and stepped inside. The window-shutters were closed. All was cool, dark, and filled with sweet scents. At first she could see nothing, being dazzled by the light from which she had just come. Something brushed against her ankles, frightening her. But when she heard a soft purring, she was greatly relieved that it was Deliverance's kitten. With great curiosity she looked around the room, which she had never before entered. Under the window a long board served as a work-table. It held a variety of bowls, measuring spoons, and bottles. In the centre was a very large bowl, covered by a plate. She lifted the cover and peered in, but instantly clapped the plate on again. A nauseating odour had arisen from the black liquid it contained. Hastily Abigail closed the door that the terrible fumes might not escape into the kitchen. She now perceived close by the bowl a parchment, which was written upon with black ink and stamped with a scarlet seal. With fingers that trembled at their daring, she put the parchment in her pocket. As she turned to go she screamed, unmindful in her fright that she might be heard.

For, from a dark corner, there jumped at her a witch in the form of a toad.

Now it is all very well for a little maid to stand still and scream when assailed by a witch, but when a second and a third, a fourth, a fifth, and even a sixth witch appear, hopping like toads, it behooves that little maid to stop screaming and turn her attention to the best plan of removing herself from their vicinity. So Abigail fran-

tically stepped upon a stool and thence to
the table.   Then she looked down.   She
saw the six witches squatted in a row on
the floor, all looking up at her, blinking
their bright eyes.   They had such a knowing and mischievous air that she felt a yet
greater distance from them would be more
acceptable.   With an ease born of long
experience in climbing trees, she swung
herself to the rafter above the table.   Her
feet, hanging over, were half concealed by
the bunches of dried herbs tied to the
beams.   She had no sooner seated herself
as comfortably as possible, when she heard
footsteps and the tap of a walking-stick in
the kitchen.   Another moment and the
door opened, and Sir Jonathan Jamieson
put his head inside.

"Are you in, Master Wentworth?" he
asked.   Receiving no reply he stepped
inside.   He lifted the cover from the large
bowl and instantly recoiled.   "Faugh,"
he muttered, "the stuff has a sickish
smell."   He searched the table, even
peered into the pockets of Master Wentworth's dressing-gown hanging on the wall.

Abigail, holding her small nose tightly, silently prayed. The dust she had raised from the herbs made her desire to sneeze.

Suddenly Sir Jonathan sneezed violently.

" Kerchew," came a mild little echo.

" Kerchew!" sneezed Sir Jonathan again.

" Kerchew," went Abigail in instant imitation.

" Kerchew!" sneezed Sir Jonathan, more violently than ever this third time.

" Kerchew," followed Abigail.

Sir Jonathan glanced around suspiciously at this last distinct echo. But he saw nothing unusual. He poked the toad witches with his stick. " Scat!" said he, and they all jumped back into their dark corners. After some further searching, he went out muttering to himself.

Abigail could see him through the open door pacing up and down the kitchen, awaiting Master Wentworth. But at last growing impatient he went away.

Abigail, not daring to get down, quivered at every sound, fearing it was Master Wentworth returning. An appetizing

odour of the pumpkin was wafted to her.
She was indeed in a quandary now.   If
she descended, how should she escape the
witches?   If she let the pumpkin burn,
she would have to explain how it happened
to the goodwife.   She sniffed anxiously.
Surely the pumpkin was scorching.   All
housewifely instinct aroused, she descended,
and with a shudder at encountering the
witches, bounded from the room, slam-
ming the door after her.

She was just in time to save the pumpkin.   She added some butter and sweetening and a pretty pinch of ginger.   While
thus engaged, Master Wentworth returned.
He greeted her kindly, not observing the
goodwife's absence, and seated himself at
the table to sort his herbs.

But Abigail noticed he did not touch
them, only sat quietly, shading his eyes
with his hand.

The silence was broken by a scratching
at the still-room door.

Master Wentworth rose and opened it,
and the kitten walked out purring, its tail
proudly erect.

There are various ways of banishing indiscreet witches who assume the form of toads.

"It is strange how it came in there," remarked Master Wentworth, mildly; "the goodwife seldom enters."

Abigail, with guiltily red cheeks, stirred the pumpkin briskly. But when she glanced again at her host, she perceived he was thinking neither of her nor of the kitten. She could not know, however, that his eyes, fixed in a far-away gaze, seemed to see the green and sunken grave, blue with innocents and violets, where Deliverance's mother slept.

"Master Wentworth," Abigail summoned up courage to ask, "would ye mind biding here alone until the goodwife returns?"

"Nay," he answered, "I mind it not."

"And would ye be above giving the pumpkin a stir once in awhile?" she ventured timidly. And as he nodded assent, she put the spoon in his hand and left him.

When Goodwife Higgins returned, weary, disappointed that she could not obtain the hearing of the magistrates,—who were in court,—she found Master Wentworth sitting as in a dream, the spoon in his hand and the odour of burning pumpkin filling the air.

"The naughty baggage!" muttered the goodwife; "just wait till I clap eyes on her."

The following day the disappearance of Abigail Brewster caused general consternation in Salem Town. She had left home early in the morning for school. Several boys asserted having seen her in Prison Lane. No further traces of her were found. Many villagers had seen evil spirits in the guise of Frenchmen and Indians lurking in the surrounding forest; and when by night the child was still missing, it was popularly believed that one of these evil spirits had borne the little maid away.

Meanwhile the object of this anxiety was trudging serenely the path to Boston Town, carrying her shoes and stockings, her petticoat turned up to her knees, there being many fordways to cross.

Chapter XII

Mr. Cotton Mather visits Deliverance

NOW, upon the very day of Abigail's disappearance, ye godly minister of Boston Town, Mr. Cotton Mather, was in Salem in attendance upon the trial of an old woman, whose spectre had appeared to several people and terrified them with horrible threats. Furthermore, the Beadle had testified to having seen her "Dead Shape" lurking in the very pulpit of the church. It was with unusual relish Cotton Mather had heard her condemnation to death, considering her crime, in particular, deliberate treason to the Lord.

As he stepped from the hot and dusty court into the fresh air, salt with the sea and bright with the sunshine, a great rush of gladness filled his heart, and he mentally framed a prayer that with God's assistance he might rid this fair, new land of witches, and behold the church of his fathers firmly established. Leaving his horse for the present where it was tied to the hitching-post, outside the meeting-house, he walked slowly down the village street to the inn, there to have luncheon before setting out for Boston Town.

The fruit trees growing adown the street were green, and cast little clumps of shadow on the cobblestone pavement. And he thought of their fruitage—being minded to happy thoughts at remembrance of duty done—in the golden autumn, when the stern Puritans held a feast day in thanksgiving to the Lord.

All the impassioned tenderness of the poet awoke in him at the sight of these symbolical little trees.

"And there are the fair fruit trees," he murmured, "and also the trees of emptiness."

Now he bowed to a group of the gossips knitting on a door-stoop in the sun, and now he stooped to set upon its feet a little child that had fallen. At the stocks he dispelled sternly a group of boys who were tickling the feet of the writhing prisoners.

Thus, in one of the rarely serene moments of his troubled life, he made his leisurely way.

But only his exalted mood, wrapping him as an invisible, impenetrable garment, enabled him to pass thus serenely.

To every one else a weight of terror hung like a pall. The awful superstition seemed in the very air they breathed. How unnatural the blue sky! What a relief to their strained nerves would have been another mighty storm ! Then might they have shrieked the terror which possessed them, but now the villagers spoke in whispers, so terrible the silence of the bright noonday.   And many, although aware of the fact that the evil spirits were mostly abroad at night, yet longed for the darkness to come and cover them.   No man dared glance at his neighbour. From one cottage came the cry of a babe yet in swaddling clothes, deserted by its panic-stricken mother, who believed it possessed by an evil spirit.

Yet, mechanically the villagers pursued their daily duties.

At the tavern, Cotton Mather found Judge Samuel Sewall and the schoolmaster — who acted as clerk in court — conversing over their mugs of sack. Pleased to fall in with such company, he drew his stool up to their table.

"Alas, my dear friend," said the good judge, "this witchery business weighs heavy on my soul! I cannot foresee an end to it, and know not who will next be cried out upon. 'Tis a sorry jest, I wot, but meseemeth, in time, the hangman will be the only man left in this afflicted township. E'en my stomach turns 'gainst my best loved dishes."

On the younger man's serene, almost exalted face came a humanizing gleam of gentle ridicule. "Then indeed has the Lord used this witchery business to one godly purpose, at least, if you do turn from things of the flesh, Samuel." A rare sweetness, born of the serenity of his mind and his friendship, was in his glance.

"Nay, nay," spoke the good judge,

gruffly, "'tis an ill conscience and an haughty stomach go together. No liking have I for the man who turns from his food. Alas, that such a man should be I and I should be such a man!" he groaned. "The face of that child we condemned troubles me o' nights."

A menacing frown transformed Cotton Mather's face, and he was changed from the genial friend into the Protestant priest, imperious in his decisions. He struck his hand heavily on the table. "Shall we, then, be wrought upon by a round cheek and tender years, and shrink from doing the Lord's bidding? Most evil is the way of such a maid, and more to be dreaded than all the old hags of Christendom."

"Ay," joined in the schoolmaster, "most evil is the way of such a maid! Strange rumours are afloat regarding her. 'Tis said, that for the peace of the community she cannot be hanged too soon. 'Tis whispered that the glamour of her way has e'en cast a spell on the old jailer. Moreover, the woman of Ipswich, who was hanged a fortnight ago, did pray that the witch-maid be saved. Now 'tis an unco uncanny thing, as all the world knows, that one witch should desire good to another witch."

Cotton Mather turned a terrible glance upon the great judge. "O fool!" he cried, "do you not perceive the work of the Devil in all this? The woman of Ipswich would have had the witch-maid saved that her own black spirit might pass into this fair child's form, and thus, with double force, working in one body, the two witches would wreak evil on the world."

" Nay, nay," protested the judge, " my flesh is weaker than my willing spirit, and, I fear me, wrought upon by a fair seeming and the vanity of outward show. But we must back to court, my good friend," he added, addressing the schoolmaster.

So the two arose and donned their steeple-hats and took their walking-sticks, and arm-in-arm they went slowly down the middle of the street.

Cotton Mather, as he lunched, became

absorbed in troubled thought. The conviction grew that it was his duty to investigate to the full and personally these rumours of the witch-maid. Also, he would seek to lead her to confession to the salvation of her own soul, and, further, that he might learn something regarding the evil ways of witches, and by some good wit turn their own methods against them to the establishment of the Lord.

Full of eager resolve, he did not finish his luncheon, but left the tavern and proceeded to the jail.

There he had the old jailer open the door of the cell very softly, that he might, by some good chance, surprise the prisoner in evil doing.

Quietly the old jailer swung open the door.

Cotton Mather saw a little maiden seated on a straw pallet, knitting. Some wisps of the straw clung to her fair hair, some to her linsey-woolsey petticoat. Where the iron ring had slipped on her white ankle was a red mark.

All the colour went from Deliverance's

face as she looked up and perceived her visitor. Before his stern gaze she trembled, and her head drooped, and she ceased her knitting. The ball of yarn rolled out from her lap over to the young minister's feet.

She waited for him to speak. The moments passed and still he did not speak, and the torture of his silence grew so great that at last she lifted her head and met his glance, and out of her pain she was enabled to speak. "What would ye have with me, good sir?"

"I have come to pray with you, and to exhort you to confession," he answered.

"Nay, good sir," protested Deliverance, "I be no witch."

The old jailer entered with a stool for Mr. Mather, and having set it down, went out and left the two together.

Ere either could speak, there was a rapping at the door.

In answer to the young minister's summons to enter, Sir Jonathan Jamieson came in.

Deliverance glanced dully at him, all

uncaring; for she felt he had harmed her all he could, and now might nevermore injure her.

The young minister, having much respect for Sir Jonathan, rose and begged that he be seated. But Sir Jonathan, minded to be equally polite, refused to deprive Mr. Mather of the stool. So they might have argued and bowed for long, had not the jailer appeared with another stool.

"I did but see you enter now, as I chanced to come out of the tavern near by," remarked Sir Jonathan, seating himself comfortably, leaning back against the wall, "and, being minded to write a book upon the evil ways of witchery, I followed you in, knowing you came to exhort the prisoner to repentance. So I beg that you will grant me the privilege to listen in case she should confess, that I may thereby obtain some valuable notes." As he spoke he shot a quick glance at Deliverance.

She could not divine that menacing look. Was he fearful lest she should confess, or did he indeed seek to have her do so?

Cotton Mather turned, his face filled with passionate and honest fervour, toward the speaker.

"Most gladly," he answered with hearty sympathy; "it is a noble and useful calling. I oft find more company with the dead in their books than in the society of the living, and it has ever been one of my chief thanksgivings that the Lord blessed me with a ready pen. But more of this later. Let us now kneel in prayer."

They both knelt.

But Deliverance remained seated.

"Wicked and obstinate o' heart I be," she said, "but Sir Jonathan holds me from prayer. I cannot kneel in company with him."

She no longer felt any fear to speak her mind.

At her words Cotton Mather glanced at Sir Jonathan and saw the man's face go red. His suspicions were aroused thereat, and he forgot all his respect for Sir Jonathan's great position and mickle gold, and spoke sternly, as became a minister, recognizing in his profession neither high nor low.

"Do you indeed exercise a mischievous spell to hold this witch-maid from prayer when she would seem softened toward godliness?"

"Nay," retorted Sir Jonathan, "'tis the malice of her evil, invisible spectre whispering at her ear to cast a reflection on me."

"I prithee go, however, and stand in the corridor outside, and we will see if the witch-maid, relieved of your presence, will pray," advised Cotton Mather.

Sir Jonathan was secretly angered at this command, yet he rose with what fair show of grace he could muster, and went out into the corridor. But an indefinable fear had sprung to life in his heart. For, lo, but a look, a word, an accusation, and one was put upon as a witch.

Deliverance, although she feared the young minister, yet knew him to be not only a great but a good man, and desirous for her soul's good. Thus willingly she knelt opposite him.

Long and fervently he prayed. Meanwhile, Sir Jonathan sauntered up and down the corridor, swinging his blackthorn stick lightly, humming his Old World tune.

Every time he passed the open door, he cast a terrible glance at Deliverance over the minister's kneeling figure, so that she shuddered, feeling she was indeed besieged by the powers of darkness on one hand, and an angel of light on the other.

Cotton Mather could not see those terrible glances, but even as he prayed, he was conscious of Sir Jonathan's unconcerned humming and light step. This implied some disrespect, so that it was with displeasure he called upon him to return.

"I cannot understand, Sir Jonathan," he remarked, rising and resuming his seat, "how it is that you who are so godly a man, should exercise a spell to hold this witch-maid from prayer."

Sir Jonathan shrugged his shoulders.

"She has a spectre which would do me evil. 'Tis a plot of the Devil's to put reproach on me, in that I have refused to do his bidding." An expression of low cunning came into his glance. "Have not you had similar experience, Mr. Mather? Methinks I have heard that the tormentors of an afflicted young woman did cause your very image to appear before her."

"Yea," rejoined Mr. Mather with some heat, "the fiends did make themselves masters of her tongue, so in her fits she did complain I put upon her preternatural torments. Yet her only outcries when she recovered her senses were for my poor prayers. At last my exhortations did prevail, and she, as well as my good name, was delivered from the malice of Satan."

Sir Jonathan stooped to flick some dust off his buckled shoe with his kerchief. "One knows not on whom the accusation of witchery may fasten. Even the most godly be not spared some slander." Now when he stooped, Deliverance thought she had seen a smile flicker over his face, but when he lifted his head, his expression was deeply grave. He met the young minister's suspicious and uncomfortable glance serenely. "What most convinces me," he continued easily, "of the prisoner's guilt, e'en more than the affliction she put upon me, is the old yeoman's testimony that he saw her conversing in the woods with Satan. Could we but get to the root of that matter, perchance the whole secret may be revealed. But I would humbly suggest she tell it in my ear, alone, lest the tale prove of too terrible and scandalous a nature to reach thy pious ear. Then I would repeat it to you with becoming delicacy."

"Nay," answered Cotton Mather, "a delicate stomach deters me not from investing aught that may result to the better establishment of the Lord in this district."

Deliverance began to feel that her secret would be torn from her against her will. Alas, what means of self-defence remained to her! Her fingers closed convulsively upon the unfinished stocking in her lap. The feminine instinct to seek relief from painful thought by some simple occupation of sewing or knitting, awakened in her. She resolved to continue her knitting, counting each stitch to herself, never permitting her attention to swerve from the task, no matter what words were addressed to her.

So in her great simplicity, and innocent of all worldly conventionalities, she sought security in her knitting.

This action was so unprecedented, it suggested such quiet domesticity and the means by which good women righteously busied themselves, that both priest and layman were disconcerted, and knew not what to do.

Suddenly Sir Jonathan laughed harshly. "The witch has a spice of her Master's obstinacy," he cried. "Methinks 'twere right good wisdom, since your prayers and exhortations avail not with her, to try less gentle means and use threats," his crafty mind catching at the fact that whatever strange, but, he feared to him, familiar tale, the little maid might tell, it could be misconstrued as the malice of one who had given herself over to Satan.

"Perchance 'twould be as well," assented Cotton Mather, greatly perplexed.

Sir Jonathan shook his forefinger at Deliverance. "Listen, mistress," said he, and sought to fix her with his menacing eye.

Deliverance, counting her stitches, heeded him not.

How pale her little face! How quick the glancing needles flashed! And ever back of her counting ran an undercurrent of thought, the words of her dream, — A little life sweetly lived.

"This would I threaten you," spoke Sir Jonathan. "You have heard how old Giles Corey is to be put to death?"

The knitting-needles trembled in the small hands. Now she dropped a stitch, and now another stitch.

"And because he will say neither that he is guilty, nor yet that he is not guilty, it is rumoured that he is to be pressed to death beneath stones," continued Sir Jonathan.

A sigh of horror followed his words. The involuntary sound came from Cotton Mather, whose imaginative, highly-strung organism responded to the least touch. His eyes were fixed upon the little maid. He saw the small hands shaking so that they could not guide the needles. How small those hands, how stamped with the innocent seeming of childhood! Oh, that the Devil should take upon himself such a disguise!

"And so, if you do not confess," spoke Sir Jonathan's cold, menacing voice, "you shall not be accorded even the mercy of being hanged, but tied hands and feet, and laid upon the ground.   And the villagers shall come and heap stones on you, and I, whom you have afflicted, shall count them as they fall.   I shall watch the first stone strike you —"

A loud cry from the tortured child interrupted him.   She sprang to her feet with arms outstretched.   "And when that first stone strikes me," she cried,

"God will take me to Himself! Ye can count the stones the others throw upon me, but I shall never ken how fast they fall!"

Cotton Mather was moved to compassion. "Let us use all zeal to do away with these evil sorcerers and their fascinations, good Sir Jonathan, but yet let us deal in mercy as far as compatible with justice, lest to do any living thing torture be a reflection on our manhood." With gentleness he then addressed himself to Deliverance, who had sunk upon her pallet and covered her face with her hands. "Explain to us why the woman of Ipswich, that was hanged, did seek that you be saved."

Deliverance made no reply. Nor could he prevail upon her in any way; so, after a weary while spent in prayers and exhortations, he and Sir Jonathan rose and went away. At the threshold Cotton Mather glanced back over his shoulder at the weeping little maid.

"'This affair savours ill," he remarked, laying his hand heavily on his companion's shoulder as the two went down the corridor; "my heart turned within me, and strange feelings waked at her cry."

It was late in the afternoon. It would not be possible for the young minister to reach Boston Town until after midnight, so he decided to postpone his journey until the next day. Moreover, he rather seized at an excuse to remain for the morrow's court, having great relish in these witch-trials.

But that night Cotton Mather had a strange vision.

Chapter XIII

In the Green Forest

SELDOM has a little girl undertaken entirely alone a more perilous journey than Abigail had started upon. Salem was not more than fourteen miles from Boston Town, but the trip invariably occupied a day, owing to the many patches of spongy ground, quicksands, and streams which intersected the way. Travellers were often aided by fallen trees and natural fordways of stone. Abigail was confident of her way, having made the trip with her father. She soon discovered the original Indian path which was acquiring some semblance to a public highway. Trees had been notched, and now and then the government had nailed notices, signifying the remaining distance to the metropolis of New England. Far more serious dangers than losing her way threatened Abigail. In the wild woods lurked savages and wolves, and the wily Frenchman with unbounded influence over the cruel Indian.

When the sun was high in the heavens, Abigail ate her luncheon. To go with what she had brought she found some strawberries, the last of the season, as if they had lingered to give this little guest of the forest a rare treat, daily acquiring a richer crimson, a finer flavour.

Abigail was obliged to follow a little stream some distance before she found an available spot to lie down and drink. It was here she missed her way. Confident that she could at will regain the main path, she walked on along a ferny lane.

Nightfall found her in the heart of the forest, unwitting which way to turn. Darkness seemed to rise from the earth, enveloping all, rising, rising, until only the tops of the trees were still brightly green. Such a sense of desolation and loneliness came over her that a sob welled up in her throat. The forest encircled her, dark, impenetrable. She walked on

some distance, and at last caught a glimpse
of the white sea-sands. It looked lighter
on the water, the waves yet imprisoning
the sunlight.   Her anxious gaze was
attracted by a faint column of blue smoke
rising beyond five tall pine trees.   So
very thin was it that it was indeed surprising she had observed it.   She started
forward gladly, but even as she made her
first eager steps she drew back with a low
cry of fear.   How did she know but that
the fire was kindled by Indians or Frenchmen?   Shivering with fear, she ran back
to the forest.

"God save my soul," she murmured,
stopping to catch her breath, " here be a
pretty to-do.   Yet perchance it might
prove to be woodmen or hunters cooking
their supper, or a party of travellers, be-
lated like myself.   I doubt not 'twould
be wisdom for me to go tippy-toe and
peek at them."

She stole back near the trees and
crouched behind a clump of hazel-bushes.
It was some time before she summoned
sufficient courage to part the leaves and

look through. And her teeth chattered like little castanets. Softly her two trembling hands parted the foliage, and her brown eyes stared out.

There just beyond the five pines was a little thatched cottage, very humble, but all so neat and clean. The roof was covered with moss which, even in the twilight, gleamed like green velvet. Up one side and over the corner, trailed the dog-rose with its blush-tinted blossoms, while on both sides of the pathway flourished the wild lilies and forest ferns. In the doorway stood a spinning-wheel, a stool beside it.

Abigail wrinkled her nose and sniffed. "Happen like I smell potatoes frying in the fat o' good bacon."

She walked boldly to the threshold and looked in.

An old woman, her back turned to the door, held a smoking skillet over the red coals on the hearth.

Abigail's heart leapt in her throat. Frenchmen and Indians — what were they? This old woman might be a witch.

Quickly she doubled her thumbs in her palms, and hastened to be first to address the old woman with pleasant words, — these being precautions advisable to take in dealing with witches.

" The cream o' the even to ye, goody," she said, " and I trust ye will have appetite for your potatoes and fat bacon, for my mother has taught me unless ye have relish for your food from honest toil, 'twill not nourish ye."

The old woman turned. " Ay," she answered in a cracked voice, " honest toil, honest toil, but I be old for toil. Who might ye be that comes so late o' day ? "

As she came forward, something seemed to clutch at the little maid's throat, and she could scarcely breathe.

For a single yellow tooth projected on the old woman's lower lip, and she had a tuft of hair like a beard on her chin, — unmistakable signs of witchery.

Yet Abigail was troubled by misgiving, for faded and sunken as the old woman's eyes were, they were still blue as if they had once been beautiful, and they had a kindly light on beholding the little maid.

"Beshrew me, it be a maid," she cried; "ye have a fair face, sweeting. How come ye here alone at the twilight hour?"

"I come from Salem, and I be bound for Boston Town," answered Abigail, timidly.

"It be good to see a bonny face," replied the old woman; "take the bucket and fetch fresh water from the spring back o' the five pines. Ay, but it be good to see a human face, to hear a young voice, and the sound o' young feet. Haste, little one, whilst I cook another flapjack, which ye shall have wi' a pouring o' molasses."

Abigail proceeded to the spring, joyful at the avenue of escape open to her. She planned to fill the bucket, leave it by the spring, and run away. But as she lifted the bucket to the stone ledge, the effort took all her strength. She could not help but think how like a dead weight it would seem to the old woman, with her bent back, when, finding that her guest did not return, she would hobble down to the spring. Strangely enough, the old woman seemed to her like a witch one moment, and the next reminded her of her own dear old Granny Brewster. So with a prayer in her heart, she carried the bucket up and set it down on the stoop, just without the threshold. There, as she had first seen her, stood the old woman cooking a flapjack, with her back turned to the door.

"It smells uncommon relishing for a witch-cake," murmured Abigail, remembering with distaste the corn-bread in her pocket. She pictured to herself the old woman's disappointment, when she should find her guest stolen away. Although possessed by fear, pity stirred within her breast, and, moved by a generous impulse, she put her hand in the front of her dress and drew forth a precious, rose-red ribbon with which she had intended to adorn herself when she reached Boston Town, and laid it on the threshold, near the bucket. Then, with an uncontrollable sob at this sacrifice, she ran swiftly away.

"Strangely enough, the old woman
seemed like a witch"

page 213

She heard the old woman calling after her to stop. Not daring to turn around, and ceasing to run, lest doing so should betray her fear, she doubled her thumbs in her palms and began to sing a psalm. Loudly and clearly she sang, the while she felt the hair rising on her head, fearing that she heard the old woman coming up behind her. Desperately she looked back. Still, very faintly in the deepening dusk, could she see the little old woman standing in the doorway, while from her hands fluttered the rose-red ribbon. And as the voice of an angel singing in the wilderness, Abigail's singing floated back to her dull ears.

    " He gently-leads mee, quiet-waters bye
      He dooth retain my soule for His name's sake
      inn paths of justice leads-mee-quietly.
      Yea, though I walke inn dale of deadly-shade
      He feare none yll, for with mee 'Thou wilt bee
      Thy rod, thy staff, eke they shall comfort mee."

Abigail walked rapidly, glad to leave the little hut and its lonely inmate far behind.

The night was upon her. Where could she seek safety? Her anxiety increased as the shadows deepened.

Alarmed, she looked around her for the safest place in which to pass the night. At first she thought of sleeping near the sea, on the warm sands. But she could not find her way out of the woods. Suddenly, on the edge of a marsh, she spied a deserted Indian wigwam. Near by were the ashes of recent fires, and a hole in the ground revealed that the store of corn once buried there had been dug up and used. Into this wigwam she crept for protection. Terrified, she watched the night descend on the marsh, which, had she but known it, was a refuge for all gentle and harmless animals and birds. Fallen trees were covered with moss, the lovely maiden-hair fern, lichens, and gorgeous fungi. The purple flag, and the wild crab, and plum trees grew here, as well as the slender red osiers, out of which the Indian women made baskets. Ere twilight had entirely vanished, Abigail saw brilliantly plumaged birds flying

back to the marsh for the night. A fox
darted into the dusk past the wigwam.
To her, nothing in all this was beautiful.
Crouched in the wigwam, she saw through
the opening white birches, like ghosts
beckoning her. A wild yellow canary, with
a circling motion, dropped into its nest.
Abigail shuddered and breathed a prayer
against witchery. Will-o'-the-wisps flashed
and vanished like breaths of flame, and
she thought they were the lanterns of
witches out searching for human souls.

As night now settled in good earnest,
a stouter heart than this little Puritan
maiden's would have quailed. The terrible howling of wolves arose, mingling
with the mournful tu-whit-tu-whoo of the
owls and the croaking of the bull-frogs.
She was in constant dread lest she might
be spied upon by Indians, who, according
to the Puritan teachings, were the last of
a lost race, brought to America by Satan,
that he might rule them in the wilderness,
undisturbed by any Christian endeavours
to convert them.

On the opposite edge of the marsh,

a tall hemlock pointed to a star suspended like a jewel just above it.

When, in after years, Abigail became a dear little old lady, she used to tell her grandchildren of the strange fancy that came into her mind as she watched that star. For, as she said, it was so soft and yellow, and yet withal so bright, that it seemed to be saying as it looked down at her:—

"Here we are, you and I, all alone in these wild woods; but take courage. Are we not together?"

A sweet sense of companionship with the star stole over her, and she was no longer lonely. She found herself smiling back at this comrade, so bright and merry and courageous. Thus smiling, she passed into the deep slumber, just recompense of a good heart and honest fatigue.

When she awoke, the sun was shining. Hastily she drew off her shoes and stockings, which she had worn during the night for warmth. Then as her eyes, still heavy with sleep, comprehended the beauty of the marsh, she was filled with delight.

The sun sent shafts of golden light into

the cool shade. All the willows and slender fruit trees glistened with morning dew. The pools of water and the green rushes rippled in the morning breeze. The transparent wings of the dragon-fly flashed in the blue air. All the birds twittered and sang. Beyond, the solemn pines guarded the secret beauties of the marsh. Thus that which had filled her with terror in the darkness, now gave her joy in the light.

By the height of the sun she judged she must have slept late and that she must make all haste to reach Boston Town in time. It was not long before she struck the main path again.

Great was her astonishment and delight to learn by a sign-board, nailed to a tall butternut tree, that she was within little over an hour's walk from Boston Town.

This sign, printed in black letters on a white board, read as follows : —

Ye path noo Leadeth
to ye flowing River &
beyonde wich ye Toone of Boston
Lyeth. bye ye distance of 2 mls
uppe ye Pleasant Hill.

And below was written in a flowing hand : —

"Oh, stranger, ye wich are Aboute Arriv'd safe at ye End of ye dayes journey the wich is symbolical of ye Soule's Pilgrimage onn earth, Kneel ye doone onn yur Marrow Bones & Pray for ye Vile Sinner wich has miss'd ye Strait & Narrow path & peetifully Chosen ye Broad & Flowery Waye wich leadeth to Destruction & ye Jaws of Death."

Abigail read the sign over hastily and passed on. "I will get down on my marrow-bones when I come back," she murmured; "I be in mickle haste for loitering."

Soon she neared the river beyond which stretched the pleasant hill. She heard a voice singing a hymn a far distance behind her. She turned and waited until the singer should have turned the curve of the road. The singing grew louder and then died away. A little later Mr. Cotton Mather, mounted on his white horse, came in sight. It seemed to her that far as he was from her, their glances met and then he turned and looked behind him.

That moment was her salvation. Quickly she ran and hid behind the trunk of a great tree. Cotton Mather came slowly on. His horse was well nigh spent with fatigue. She saw him distinctly, his face white from exhaustion, his eyes sombre from a sleepless night. His black velvet small-clothes were spattered with mud. He reined in his horse so near her that she might almost have touched him.

He removed his hat to greet the cool river breeze. His countenance at this time of his young manhood held an irresistible ardour. Some heritage had bestowed upon him a distinction and grace, even a worldliness of mien, which, where he was unknown, would have permitted him to pass for a courtier rather than a priest. At this moment no least suggestion of anything gross or material showed in his face, which was so nearly unearthly in its exaltation that the little maid watching him was awed thereat and sank to her knees. His very presence seemed to inspire prayer.

A moment he looked searchingly around him, then spurred his horse to take the ford. She saw the bright water break around his horse's feet, the early sunshine falling aslant his handsome figure. She watched until he reached the further bank and disappeared behind a gentle hill. Then she came out from her hiding.

When in after years she beheld him, — his public life a tragedy by reason of his part in the witchcraft trouble and his jealous strivings to maintain the infallibility of the Protestant priesthood, — saw him mocked and ridiculed and slaves named after him, a vision would rise before her. She would see again that magnificent young figure on the white horse, the radiant air softly defining it amidst the greenness of the forest, herself a part of the picture, a little child kneeling hidden behind a tree in the early morning.

The fordway was so swollen that Abigail did not dare attempt to cross on foot. And although further down where the river narrowed and deepened there was a ferryman, she had not the money with which to pay toll. Thinking, however, that it would not be long before some farm people would be going into town with their produce, she sat down on the shore and dabbled her feet in the cold water to help pass away the time. At last when the first hour had passed, and she was waxing impatient, there appeared, ambling contentedly down the green shadowed road, a countryman on his fat nag, his saddle-bags filled with vegetables and fruit for market.

Abigail rose. "Goodman," said she, "would ye be so kind as to take me across the river? I be in an immoderate haste."

"To be sure," said the countryman; "set your foot on my boot; let me have your shoes and stockings. Give me your hands. Now, jump; up we go, that's right. Ye be an uncommon vigorous lassie."

The horse splashed into the water, which rose so high that Abigail's bare feet and ankles and the farmer's boots were wet. The little maid put her arms as far as she could reach around her companion's broad waist, and clung tightly to him, her little teeth firmly set to keep from screaming as the horse rolled and slipped on the stones in the river bed.

When they reached the other side, Abigail, desperately shy, insisted upon her companion permitting her to dismount, although he offered to carry her all the way into town.

" Ye be sure ye can find your home, child ? " he asked, loath to leave her.

Abigail nodded and sat down on the ground to pull on her shoes and stockings, while the countryman after a moment's further hesitation made his way leisurely up the grassy hill.

After a brisk walk, Abigail arrived at Boston Common, a large field in which cows were pastured during the daytime, and where, in the evening, the Governor and his Lady and the gallants and their

"Marmalet Madams" strolled until the nine o'clock bell rang them home and the constables began their nightly rounds. The trees that once covered the Common had been cut down for firewood, but there were many thickets and grassy knolls. On one side the ground sloped to the sea where the cattle wandered through the salt marsh grasses. And there was to be heard always the sweet incessant jangle of their bells. At this hour of the morning there was generally to be seen no person except the herdsman, but as Abigail approached a stately elm which stood alone in the field, she saw a student lying on the grass, reading.

Chapter XIV

A Fellow of Harvard

HIS book lay open between his elbows, and his chin was propped on his hands. His cap lay on the grass near by.

Abigail's shyness tempted her to hurry by him without attracting attention, but when she remembered that he might know something of the fine gentleman she was seeking, she paused bravely.

"It will be a fair day, sir," she said in a quavering voice.

The young man rolled over on his elbow. He wore no wig, and his lank dark hair, parted in the centre, fell on either side of his long, colourless face. His eyes were sharp and bright.

"On what authority dare you make so rash a statement?" inquired he, sternly. "Take heed how you say such things, lest it rain and thunder and the wind blow, and a hurricane come upon us this afternoon, and you be prosecuted for telling a falsehood."

Abigail failed to perceive he was but jesting, and this, as well as timidity and anxiety, so wrought upon her, that without further ado she began to cry.

At this the student jumped up, deeply repentant, and entreated her to rest in the shade of the old elm tree by him. He gave her his kerchief to dry her eyes, and offered an apple from his pocket.

" 'There, there," he said, " 'twas but an idle jest. I am a bit of a merry-andrew in my way, but a harmless fellow, without a grain of malice in me. Sure the sun will shine all day when the morn is fair like this. Look up, my pretty lass. See, it still shines."

Abigail obediently blinked her tear-wet lashes at the dazzling sun, then turned her attention to the apple. She ate it with great relish, the while the student leant back against the tree, his hands in his pockets and his long legs crossed. Thus leisurely reclining, he sang a song for her pleasure, such as never before had greeted her staid, religious little ears. His voice was wondrous mellow, and its cadences flung over her a charmed spell.

> " It was a lover and his lass,
>   With a hey and a ho and a hey-nonino,
> That o'er the green corn fields did pass
>   In the spring-time, the only pretty ring-time
> When birds do sing, hey-ding-a-ding, ding,
>   Sweet lovers love the spring."

" Beshrew me," remarked Abigail, taking a bite of her apple, "but ye sing strange songs in Boston Town."

"Did ye ne'er hear tell of Willie Shakespeare, the play-actor," cried the student. " I am amazed, sore amazed, at your ignorance. Many a rare rhyme has he written, God rest his bones, and betwixt you and me, I, as a Fellow of Harvard, privileged to be learned, find that there are times when his poesy rings with more relish in my ears than the psalms. I have tried my hand at verse-making with fair fortune, though I say it as should not." Then he burst forth into another rollicking song :—

> "Full fathoms five thy father lies;
>   Of his bones are coral made;
>   Those are pearls that were his eyes:
>   Sea-nymphs hourly ring his knell —"

" Beshrew me, sir," interrupted Abigail, her disapproval too strong to be repressed, " but these songs are not to my liking." She rose. " I will be pleased to have you read this description, sir," she said, drawing a paper from her pocket tied by a string around her waist, " and tell me if ye ken aught o' this fine gentleman."

The student rose and made her a low bow. " Since you be pleased to put on such dignity, mistress," said he, with a fine and jesting air, " I must needs fall in with your ways."

He took the paper she extended to him and unfolded it with many airs, the while crooking his little fingers daintily.

This was what he read, written in a fair and flowing hand as did befit a teacher of the Dame School : —

" A descripshun of ye fine gentellman whom I met in ye forest on ye afternoon of June 3 wich is herein sett downe.   He be aboute three score more or less

& be of make suffishunt large to be stared att & for ye naughty boys of ye streete to call att, he having an immoderate goodly girth arounde ye middle. shure did yu know him yu would be of my minde that he had grate rank across ye seas fore he wears full breeches with knots of ryban of a Purple-Blue colour att his knees. alsoe he do walke inn grate bootes. his Sleeves be of fine Velvet withe watchet-Blue Tiffany peeping through ye Slashes. alsoe he carried a blacke case bestock with smal sharp knives exceeding bright. he showed me a picture of his lyttle maide of faire countenance. As regardes ye countenance of ye fine gentellman itt was wrighte goode to looke att having Witte Beauty & Goodness, as theay say. alsoe he weares a light Brown Wigg, parted to ye Crown & falling in Naturall Silke curles to his Shoulders. his Moustache curls finely towards his Nose.

by ye wich descripshun Abigail finde him & deliver ye pckge soe saye I & ye Lord be willing.

Deliverance Wentworth.

note. alsoe he weares a sword."

"Well-a-day!" laughed the student as he finished, "this is a pretty joke."

"It be no joke at all, sir," said Abigail, "and ye will pardon my frowardness in contradicting ye, for my dear friend Deliverance will be hanged o' Saturday for witchery." And putting the kerchief to her eyes she wept afresh.   As she did so, she heard a strange sound like a groan, and looked up quickly.

The student was leaning against the elm, his eyes closed and his face whiter than the paper which had fluttered from his fingers to the ground.

" Haps it that ye ken her, sir ? " she asked in an awed whisper.

He looked at her and tried to regain his composure.   His lips moved dumbly. He turned away and put his hand over his eyes, leaning once more against the tree. When he looked again at Abigail, she saw that tears bedimmed his eyes.   This exhibition of feeling on the part of this gay student seemed an even more serious thing than the fact that Deliverance was in jail, or that she herself had passed a night in the forest, exposed to savages and wolves.

The student, looking at the little maid's troubled, tear-stained countenance, smiled in a faint, pitiful fashion, bidding her have hope and cheer.   But his voice faltered and broke.

Something in his smile arrested Abigail's

attention. Suddenly, a light of recognition breaking over her face, she put forth her hands, crying joyfully: "Ye be Ronald. Ye be Deliverance's brother. She telled me to look for ye, but I ne'er suspicioned it to be ye. But when ye smiled I thought o' her, and now I have remembrance o' having seen ye in Salem Town."

Young Wentworth made no reply save by a groan. "Long have I misdoubted these trials for witchery," he muttered. "It tempts one to atheism. She, Deliverance, a witch, to be cast into prison! a light-hearted, careless child! God himself will pour out His righteous wrath upon her judges if they so much as let a hair of her head be harmed. They have convicted her falsely, falsely! Come," he cried, turning fiercely upon Abigail, "come, we will rouse the town! We shall see if such things can be done in the name of the law. We shall see."

Now such anger had been in his eyes as to have burned away his tears, but all at once his fierceness died and his voice broke.

"Did they treat her harshly," he

asked, — "my little sister, who since her mother died, has been a lone lassie despite her father and brother. Tell me again, again that it be not until to-morrow, — that one day yet of grace remains."

So Abigail told him all she knew. But when he desired to see the letter she was to give to the Cavalier, she protested : —

"I promised not to read it myself nor to let any other body, except him, for Deliverance said it must be kept secret, she being engaged on a service for the King. She said when I found ye, ye would go with me to look for the fine gentleman."

"Very well, we will go," he answered briefly, and took her hand, seeing that it would only trouble her then to insist upon having the letter, but resolving to obtain possession of it at the first opportunity.

"We will go to the Governor's house, first," he added, "and see if he knows the whereabouts of any such person. If not, then I must read the letter and find the clue to unravel this sad mystery."

Master Ronald walked on rapidly, holding her hand in so tight a grasp that she was obliged to run to keep up with him. They soon left the Common and entered a street. There were no sidewalks then in Boston Town. The roadways, paved with pebbles, extended from house to house. They took the middle of the street where the walking was smoothest. Once Master Ronald paused to consider a sun-dial.

"It lacks o'er an hour of ten," he said; "we shall be obliged to wait. The new Governor is full of mighty high-flown notions fetched from England, and will see no one before ten, though it be a matter of life and death. It sorts not with his dignity to be disturbed." He glanced down at Abigail as he finished speaking, and for the first time took notice that she was tired and pale.

"Have you broken fast this morn?" he inquired; "I should have bethought me of your lack. There is yet ample time, and you must eat. Come," he added, taking her hand again and smiling, "it is good for neither soul nor body that the latter should go hungered. The Queen's coffee-house lies just around yon corner."

A few moments later Abigail found herself seated at a table in a long, dark room, very quiet and cool, with vine-clad windows. Only one other customer besides themselves was in the room. He was an old gentleman in cinnamon-brown small-clothes, and he was so busy sipping a cup of coffee and reading a manuscript, that he did not glance up at their entrance. The inn-keeper's buxom wife received Master Ronald's order. Quite on her own account she brought in also a plate of cookies.

"Kiss me well, honey-sweet," said she, "and you shall have the cookies."

So Abigail kissed the goodwife in return for her gift.

"Heigh-ho!" remarked Master Ronald, "in all this worry and grief I forgot that every maid has a sweet tooth, if she be the proper sort of maid." In spite of his little pleasantry, his troubled look remained.

Abigail ate steadily, not pausing to talk, only now and then glancing at her companion. After awhile Master Ronald rose, and strode up and down with savage impatience. "Alack!" he said, "I seem to be losing my wits."

Abigail, having finished, commenced putting the remaining cookies in her pocket.

"Why do you do that?" asked Master Ronald.

"I want summat to eat on my way home," answered Abigail, resolutely, crowding in the last cooky.

The young man laughed, but his laughter ended abruptly in a sigh of pain.

Abigail could not but admire the grand and easy way in which, with a wave of his hand, he bade the inn-keeper charge the breakfast to his account, as they left the coffee-house.

He led the way back to the sun-dial. They had been gone not more than twenty minutes. Frowning, Master Ronald turned his back toward the dial and leant against it. "We may as well stop

here," said he, "and wait for the minutes
to speed."

Abigail pushed away the vines to read
the motto printed on the dial. "'I marke
the Time; saye, gossip, dost thou soe,'"
she read unconsciously aloud.

"Time," echoed Master Ronald, catching the word, "time." He shrugged
his shoulders. "What is more perverse
than time? It takes all my philosophy
to bear with it, and I oft wonder why
'twas e'er put in the world. 'Tis like a
wind that blows first hot then cold. It
must needs stand still when you most wish
it to speed, and when you would fain have
it stand still, it goes at a gallop." He
sighed profoundly and kicked a pebble
with the toe of his shoe.

His expression was so miserable that
Abigail's ready tears flowed again in sympathy, so that she was obliged to pick up
the hem of her petticoat and wipe them
away. Her attention was suddenly attracted by noisy singing and much merriment. She dropped her petticoat.
"Happen like there be a dancing-bear in
town?" she asked eagerly.

"Nay," answered Master Ronald, "'tis some of my fellows at the tavern, who have been suspended a day for riotous conduct."

"Come, come," cried he, taking her almost fiercely by the hand. There was a new ring in his voice, a sudden strong resolve shining in his face. He led her along the road in the direction from which the sounds proceeded, and paused at last in front of a tavern which had as a sign a head of lettuce painted in red. From this place came the singing.

Master Ronald, still holding her hand, swung the door open and stepped inside with her. As her eyes became accustomed to the dim light she perceived some eight or ten young fellows with lank locks falling about their faces, seated around a large bowl of hasty pudding, into which bowl they dipped their spoons. Two or three who were perched on the table, however, had ceased eating, and were smoking long brier-wood pipes. They did not perceive Master Ronald and Abigail. Suddenly they all lifted

high their mugs of sack and broke into
song.

> " Where the red lettuce doth shine,
> 'Tis an outward sign,
> Good ale is a traffic within.
> It will drown your woes
> And thaw the old snow
> That grows on a frosty chin,
> That grows on a frosty chin."

" Enough, enough, sirs!" Master Ronald cried sharply; "down with your mugs!
Are ye to drink and be merry when murder — murder, I say — is being done in
the name of the church and the law?"

The students turned in open-mouthed
amazement, several still holding their
mugs suspended in the air. At first
they were evidently disposed to be merry
as people accustomed to all manner of
jesting, but the pallor and rigid lines of
the young man's face checked any such
demonstration, as well as the unusual appearance of a little maid in their midst.

Then one tall and powerful fellow rose.
" Murder," he said slowly, shaking back

his hair, "murder — under sanction of the church and law.   How comes that?"

Master Ronald made a gesture commanding silence, for the others had risen, and a confused hubbub of questions was rising.   Then he pointed to Abigail, who was near to sinking to the floor with mortification, as all eyes were turned upon her.

"This little maid," he continued, when the room was again silent, "journeyed alone from Salem to Boston Town, to find and tell me that in Salem prison there is confined another maid condemned for witchery and under sentence of being hanged on the morrow."

His words were interrupted by groans and hisses.

"A plague upon these witch-trials," cried one of his hearers; "a man dare not glance askance at his neighbour, fearing lest he be strung up for sorcery.   And now 'tis a maid.   Lord love us!   Are they not content with torturing old beldames?"

There came a flash into the eyes of the

stalwart youth who had first spoken. "'Tis not so long a journey to Salem Town but we might make it in a night."

An answering flash lit the eyes of his fellows as they nodded and laughed at the thought which, half-expressed, showed in the faces of all. But they grew quiet as Master Ronald began speaking once more.

"'Tis a matter of life and death. The imprisoned maid is near the age of this little maid, as innocent, as free from guile —." He broke down and dropped into a chair, folded his arms on the table, and buried his face in them while his shoulders shook with repressed grief.

The rest, troubled and embarrassed by his emotion, drew together in a little group and talked in low tones.

"Perchance 'tis a relation, a sister," commented one young man, "a maid, he said, like yonder little lass;" and the speaker indicated Abigail, who had edged over to the door and stood, with burning face, nervously fingering her linsey-woolsey petticoat.

"I have no patience with these, our

godly parsons," cried another student, who wore heavily bowed spectacles. "I have here a composition, which with great pains I have set down, showing how weak are the proofs brought against those accused of witchery." He took off and breathed on his spectacles and wiped them on his kerchief. Then, having replaced them on his nose, he drew a written paper out of his pocket and unfolding it began to read aloud.

But he was interrupted impatiently by the rest. "'Tis no time for words but action, Master Hutchinson," they cried, giving him the prefix to his name, for these young Cambridge men called each other "Master" and "Sir" with marked punctiliousness.

"It behooves me 'twere well to inquire into the merits of this case, but I am loath to disturb him," said one bright-eyed young man, whom his fellows called Philander, glancing at Master Ronald's bowed head. "Ah, I have it!" he cried, clapping the man nearest him on the shoulder; "we'll not disturb his moping-fit but let him have it out. Meanwhile we'll make inquiry of this little maid."

As he drew near Abigail, she, startled, flew to Master Ronald's side and shook him. "Oh, sir," she cried, "wake up! They are going to speer me."

At this the gravity of the young men relaxed into laughter so hearty that even Master Ronald, looking up, comprehended the situation and smiled faintly.

"They are less amusing and more dangerous than dancing-bears, eh, Mistress Abigail?" he asked, rising to his feet.

Abigail did not commit herself by replying. "Let us haste away, sir," she said; "bethink yourself how Deliverance waits, and you will pardon my rudeness, but, sir, it be no time now for a moping-fit."

"Bravo!" cried Master Philander, "there is the woman of it. You prefer to do your duty first and have your weep afterwards."

"I will take you to see the Governor in a moment, Mistress Abigail," said Master Ronald; "we will be there prompt on the moment. There is that whereof I would speak to my friends who are bound to any cause of mine, as I to theirs, in all loyalty, when that cause be just."

At this the students interrupted him by shouts, but he raised his hand to silence them. "Hear me to the end without interruption, as the time waxes short. In Salem, my fair young sister, scarce more than a child in years, languishes in jail, for having, it is asserted, practised the evil art of witchery. On the morrow she will be hanged, unless, by the grace of God, the Governor may be prevailed upon to interfere. If he refuses justice and mercy, then have we the right to take the law into our own hands, not as trespassers of the law, but rather as defenders of law and justice. As men sworn to stand by each other, how many of you will go with me to Salem Town this night and save the life of one as innocent and brave, as free from evil, as this maid who stands before you now?"

There was no shouting this time, but silently each young man moved over and shook hands with the speaker in pledge of his loyalty and consent.

" And now," added Master Ronald, " I will go to the Governor's house, that you may have your say with him, Mistress Abigail."

" We will escort you there," said the stalwart young fellow Abigail had first noticed. Before she could protest, to her indignation he had seized her and swung her up on his broad shoulder, passed her arm around his neck, and rested her feet on his broad palm.

" Now I have placed you above learning, little mistress," he cried gayly ; " duck your head as we go through the door."

Abigail clasped his neck tightly, and lifted up her heart in prayer. Intense was her mortification to observe how the people turned and looked after them. She grew faint at the thought of her father's awful, pious eye beholding her.

" They may be much for learning," she murmured, glancing over the heads of the students, " but, beshrew me, they be like a pack o' noisy boys. Oh, Deliverance, Deliverance, how little ye kenned this torment ! "

Q

Chapter XV

Lord Christopher Mallett

DOWN many a crooked street and round many a corner, the crowd of students bore her, until at last they reached the Governor's place, "a faire brick house" on the corner of Salem and Charter streets.

Above the doorway were the King's arms richly carved and gilded. Some stone steps led down the sloping lawn to the street, which was shut out by a quaint wooden fence.

Here, at the lanterned gateway, the student who carried Abigail set her down upon the ground.

"Come, Mistress Abigail," said Master Ronald, holding the gate open for her to pass in.

Once safely inside Abigail did not forget her manners, but turned about, spread out her petticoat, and courtesied to all the merry young gentlemen, who, leaning over the gate, smiled and doffed their caps.

Then retying the strings of her bonnet primly under her chin, and giving her skirts a flirt, she walked with Master Ronald to the door.

Master Ronald raised the knocker and rapped thrice vigorously.

The door was opened by an old Moor, — so was the negro called by the good folk of those days. When he beheld the student he smiled and bowed ; then with deprecating gesture fell to shaking his head solemnly.

"Don't concern yourself this time, Pompey," said the student, grimly. "I have other business than whining for pardon. Lack-a-mercy-me ! I feel as if I should never have heart for any more quips or pranks. Is his Excellency in ? Tell him that Ronald Wentworth, a Fellow of Harvard, awaits his pleasure."

The negro ushered them into the hall-room and placed a stool for Abigail. The little maid perched herself stiffly upon it

and gazed around her, greatly awed by
the magnificence, while Master Ronald,
with his hands behind him clasping his
cap, paced restlessly up and down the
room, his countenance so colourless and
lined with anxiety that it was like the
face of an old man. The hall into which
they had been shown served not only as a
passageway but as a living-room. From
one side the staircase, with its quaintly
carved balustrade, rose by a flight of
broad steps to the second story. In the
centre of this hall-room was a long table
laid with a rich cloth on which was placed
a decanter of wine. Stools with cushions
of embroidered green velvet were placed
for those who sat at the Governor's board.
Abigail's sharp eyes noted a spinning-
wheel in front of the fireplace, which was
set round with blue Dutch tiles. But
she was most delighted by a glimpse she
caught of the cupboard which contained
the Governor's silver plate.

The rear door of the hall was swung
open and she could see a pretty gentle-
woman working in the garden. Her

cheeks vied in richness of colour with the crimson coif she wore beneath her straight-brimmed, steeple hat, as she gathered a nosegay, the basket on her arm being filled to overflowing.

At last, Master Ronald, pausing, leant his elbow on the carved newel-post of the staircase and sighed heavily.

"Did you say Deliverance was treated with decency and kindness in jail?" he asked. "Let them but harm a hair of her pretty head and they shall have ample proof of the love I bear my little sister."

As he spoke, the door opposite opened and a gentleman came out, closing it behind him. He was a tall and solemn-visaged man, richly attired in velvet, with a sword at his side. There was that air of distinction in his bearing which made Abigail instantly surmise that she was in the presence of Sir William Phipps, the new Governor, who had arrived last month from England. He addressed her companion, taking no notice of her.

"Well, well, Master Wentworth, and that be your name," he said, "let me warn you to expect no leniency from me nor intercession on your behalf with your masters at Cambridge. I have scarce been in this miserable country two months, yet have had naught dinged in my ears but the mischievous pranks of you students of Harvard. 'Tis first the magistrates coming to complain of your roisterings and rude and idle jestings, and I no sooner have rid myself of them than you students come next, following on their very heels with more excuses than you could count, and puling and whining for mercy. But sit down, young sir, sit down," he ended, taking a seat as he spoke. He crossed his legs, put the tips of his fingers together, and leant back comfortably in his massively carved oak chair. Chairs were then found only in the houses of the very well-to-do. So it was with some pride that Sir William waved the student to the one other chair in the hall.

But Master Ronald, too nervous to remain quiet, refused impatiently. "I have come with —"

"There is too much of this book learning, nowadays," interrupted Sir William, following his own train of thought. "The more experience I have of yon Cambridge students, the more convinced I be, that three fourths should be taken out of college and apprenticed to a worthy trade. Let such extreme learning be left to scholars, lest ordinary men, being too much learned, should set themselves above their ministers in wisdom. As for myself—"

"Ay," interrupted Master Ronald, desperately, "but the matter on which I come to-day—"

"As for myself," continued Sir William, glancing severely at the student, "I started out in life apprenticed to an honest trade. From ship's carpenter, I have risen to fortune and position. But I will confess I grow that troubled with the management of this province, what with the Indian and French wars on the one hand, and this witchery business on the other, that I do often wish I might go back to my broad-axe again, where one can be an honest man with less perplexity."

"Sir," spoke the student, sharply, "I crave your pardon, but I have no time for talk to-day. 'Tis a matter —"

"Very well," retorted Sir William, annoyed, "we will hear of this very important matter, but let me warn you beforehand to expect no indulgence. So you can go on with your plaint, if you count time so poorly as to waste it on a cause already lost, for 'tis to-day I shall begin to make an example of some of you."

"I come on no private business of my own," retorted Master Ronald with spirit, "but in company with this little maid." He indicated Abigail by a wave of his hand.

She slipped down from her stool thereat and courtesied.

The Governor took no notice of her politeness beyond a severe stare. "Well," he inquired, "and for what did you come?"

"If you please, your Excellency," faltered Abigail, "Deliverance, my dear friend —"

At this, Master Ronald, who stood on the further side of the Governor's chair, coughed. She glanced up and saw he had put his finger to his lips to enjoin silence. Frightened, she stopped short.

During the pause, the Governor drew out a gold snuff-box and took a pinch of snuff. Then he flicked the powder, which had drifted on his velvet coat, off daintily with his kerchief. "Well," said he, "have you lost your tongue?"

"My dear friend, Deliverance," repeated Abigail.

"In other words," broke in Master Ronald, his tone sharp with anxiety, "she desires to ask your Excellency if you know the whereabouts of any person answering this description." And briefly he described the stranger whom Deliverance had met in the forest.

At these words the Governor's expression mellowed slightly and he smiled. "Then you have no favour to ask of me," he said. "I think I know the person of whom you speak." He rose. "I will find out if you may see him."

As he crossed the hall, he glanced out of the entrance-door which had been left half-closed.

Abigail's eyes, following the direction of his, beheld the students perched in a row on the front fence.

His Excellency turned, bestowing a grim look on Master Ronald.

"What scarecrows are those on my fence?" he asked. "I doubt not I could make better use of them in my corn-fields." And with an audible sniff he opened the door on his right and entered the room beyond.

"The Lord in his infinite justice is on our side," spoke Master Ronald, solemnly, as the door closed behind the Governor. "Praise be unto Him from whom cometh all mercy." He took a couple of long steps which brought him to Abigail's side. "Say no word of witchery to his Excellency," he whispered sternly, "lest you spoil all by a false move. Mind what I say, for he is carried away by fanaticism, and in his zeal to clear the land of witches makes no provision to spare the innocent. Hush!" He drew quickly away as steps were heard in the next room. He clasped his hands behind him and commenced pacing the floor, humming in apparent unconcern : —

"Full fathoms five thy father lies ;
  Of his bones are coral made ;
  Those are pearls that were his eyes :
    Sea-nymphs hourly ring his knell " —

Abigail fairly quaked in her shoes.

Another moment, and the door through which the Governor had passed was opened by the old Moor. He beckoned them to enter.

They found themselves in a spacious apartment, the state bed-chamber of the house.

Standing well out in the centre of the room was a great four-poster bed, with a crimson canopy. The curtains were drawn back, revealing a man lying dressed on the bed, propped up by pillows.

The Governor sat beside him. He nodded to the two young people.

"Is not this the gentleman you seek?"
he asked, with a wave of his hand toward
the occupant of the bed.

They had recognized him, however, at
once. There was the flowing wig of chestnut hue, the comely countenance, the
rich dress, the curled moustache Deliverance had so admired. One of his legs,
bound in wool and linen, rested on a
pillow. On a table at the further side
of the bed were placed some quills, an
ink-horn, and paper; also a jug of wine
and silver mugs.

"By my troth," cried this fine person,
jovially, "I expected none such pretty
visitor. Come here and kiss me, little
maiden, and I swear you shall have your
wish, whatsoe'er it be. And it be not the
round moon or the throne of England,"
he added chuckling.

Abigail courtesied at a safe distance
from the bed.

Meanwhile, Master Ronald had his eye
on Governor Phipps. He feared to mention their errand in the presence of his
Excellency, knowing that they might ex-

pect neither reason nor tolerance from him. So he drew himself up to his full height and said with confidence, not unbecoming in so learned a Fellow of Harvard : —

"Your Excellency, this is a very private and personal business." Having said this he bowed so low that his dark hair fell over his face. Thus he remained with his head deferentially bent during the moment of amazed silence which elapsed before his Excellency replied.

" I have no desire to hear," he retorted, his small eyes snapping with wrath, " but I would say unto you, young sir, that 'tis exceeding low-bred for you to be setting a lesson in manners to your elders and betters ; exceeding unfortunate and ill-bred, say I, though you be a Fellow of Harvard, where, I warrant, more young prigs flourish than in all England." With which fling his Excellency rose and left the room, followed by his servant.

" I 'gin to be fair concerned as to what this mighty business will prove to be," said the merry invalid; " my curiosity consumes me as a flame. But sit you down, little mistress, and you, young sir. You must not deem me lacking in gallantry that I rise not. Here have I lain two weeks with the gout. Was e'er such luck? But, why fret and fume, say I, why fret and fume and broil with anxiety like an eel in a frying-pan? Yet was e'er such luck as to have your thumb on your man and not be able to take him?"

"Sir," spoke Master Ronald from the stool on which he had seated himself, "we come on a matter of life and death. My sister, Deliverance Wentworth, the child you met in the forest outside Salem Town, some three weeks ago, is to be hanged on the morrow for witchery, unless by the grace of God you have power to interfere."

At these words the invalid's florid face paled, and he sank back on his pillows with a gasp of mingled horror and astonishment.

"The Lord have mercy on this evil world!" he said, wagging his head portentously. "Alack, alack! the times grow worse. What manner of men are these lean, sour Puritans that they would e'en put their babes to death for witchery? As pretty and simple a maid was she as any I e'er set eyes on, not excepting my sweetest daughter over the seas."

"Ay," said the student, raising his white face from his hands, "as sweet a maid as God e'er breathed life into. But I say this," he cried, raising his voice shrilly, in his excitement, "that if they harm her they shall suffer for it."

"Not a hair shall they hurt, and God grant me grace to live to get there," cried the invalid. "Is my word to be accounted of naught," and he tapped his breast, "mine? Oh, ho! let any dare to deny or disregard it, and he shall rue it."

"Sir," said Abigail, approaching him timidly, "Deliverance Wentworth sends ye this."

He took the package and untied the tow string which bound it. There were two papers, one the sealed parchment Abigail had found in the still-room and the other the letter Deliverance had written.

When the Cavalier saw the parchment,

he gave an inarticulate sound and clutched it to his breast, kissed it and waved it wildly.

"By my troth!" he cried, "the little maid whom they would hang, hath saved England."

In his excitement he rose, but no sooner had he put his foot on the floor, than he groaned and fell back on the bed. His face became so scarlet that Master Ronald started up, thinking a leech should be sent for to bleed him, but the sufferer waved him back, and lay down uttering praise and thanksgiving, save when he paused for groans so terrible, that Abigail jumped at every one. When he had exhausted himself and grown quiet, she, feeling it safe to approach him, summoned up courage to hand him Deliverance's letter, which had fallen from the bed to the floor.

"Ye forgot her letter," she said reproachfully.

As the Cavalier read, he swore mighty oaths under his breath, and before he finished, the tears were falling on the little letter.

"HON'D SIR: yu will indede be surprised to lern of my peetiful condishun fore I be languishing away in prison & round my ankel be an iron wring held by ye chain & itt be a grate afflictshun to ye flesh   Alle this has come uponn me since I met with yu in ye forest & olde Bartholomew Stiles wich some say be a Fule — but I would nott say of my own Accord — took yu fore Satan wich was a sadd mistake fore me.   Alsoe Goodwife Higgins mistook a yellow witch-bird & said ye same was me. I blame her nott fore I had rised betimes & gonne to ye brooke & tried onn ye golde beads & this yu will perceive I could nott tell her lest I should betray ye secret & I did give ye message to Sir Jonathan Jamieson & he saide I was a witch & alsoe Ebenezer Gibbs saide I stuck pinnes in him when I but rapped his pate fore larfing in school & intising others to Evil acts such as Twisting ye Hair of Stability Williams & fore alle this ye godly magistrates have sentenced me to be hanged wich Hon'd Sir yu will agree be a sadd afflictshun to ye flesh

As regards ye service fore ye King Abigail wich be my deare friend will give yu a pckge. but no more lest this fall into ye wrong handes when yu read this I trust yu will in Gods name come fast to Salem & take me out of prison fore I am in sore Distress & can find nothing comforting in ye Scripture, against being hanged & I beginn to feare God has not pardoned my sinnes.

Sir Jonathan Jamieson torments me most grievous & I saye unto yu Privately he be a Hypocrite & itt be Woe unto him Whited sepulchre I ken nott what he will do when he findes ye Parchment be gonne but no more lest I betray ye secret & if I should be hanged afore yu come I do heartily repent my sinnes wich I cannot set down in wrighting fore I have no more Ink. I beg with tears yu will come in time. Hon'd Sir I bewayl my ylls & peetiful condishun

DELIVERANCE WENTWORTH.

note — I hereinn putt down my will that Abigail shall have my golde beads amen

note — alsoe in Ipswich bides a hunchback whose mother be hanged fore a witch & he be named lyttel Hate-Evil Hobbs & should I be hanged I trust Hon'd Sir yu will shew him kindness fore me & now no more amen."

" Please God!" spoke the Cavalier, reverently, " Deliverance Wentworth hath done a mighty service for her King, and she shall not go unrewarded, for I am one who speaks with authority."

At these words the student looked up with a flash of hope in his eyes, and Abigail drew nearer the bed.

"Arrange the pillows under my head, little mistress," said the Cavalier, "and you, young sir, draw up the table and fill the mugs. 'Tis bad, I wot, for my leg, still a little good red wine for the stomach's sake is not to be done away with.

"And now," quoth he, solemnly, lifting high his mug, "we will drink to the health of Deliverance Wentworth, who hath done a mighty service for her King. She shall not go unrewarded, for I speak with authority. For," swelling his chest importantly, "you behold in me Christopher Mallett, Lord of Dunscomb County and Physician to his Majesty, the King."

Chapter XVI

At the Governor's House

WHILE they were still drinking, there came an imperious rap on the door. In response to Lord Christopher's bidding, the Governor entered, followed by a young minister.

Abigail was awed at the sight of the latter, recalling how she had seen him in the forest only a few short hours ago. The student put down his wine-cup and rose, deeply respectful.

"I have come to tell you, my dear friend," said the Governor, addressing himself to the Cavalier, "that a very strange miscarriage of justice calls me at once to Salem."

Ere the Cavalier could reply, his attention was diverted by the strange action of Cotton Mather, who, pausing half-way across the room, was staring at the little maid.

"I did see the spectre of that child rise before me in the forest this very morn," he cried in a curious voice.

"Nay, good sir," cried Abigail, finding voice in her terror, "it was my very living shape ye saw."

"It rose in my path," spoke Cotton Mather, as if he heard her not. "I, believing it a living child, did glance about to see who accompanied it. When I looked for it again the Shape had gone."

"Nay," cried Abigail, in mortal terror. "Nay, good sir, nay, it was my living self."

"Ay, reverend sir, it was the little maid you beheld indeed, and no Dead Shape that rose at the Devil's bidding," cried Lord Christopher, and the effect of his mellow, vigorous voice was magical. So heartily it rang that the others' thoughts of spirits and visions grew faint as those visions are disposed to be faint in flesh.

All felt it but Cotton Mather. Wrapped in his own thoughts, he still stared at the little maid.

"Do you not perceive the child is frightened to be so regarded?" cried the Cavalier, impatiently "I can swear to you, prove to you, her living self was in the forest this morning. In Salem Town, accused falsely of witchery, there languishes a little maid — "

"A little maid," cried Cotton Mather, still in his strained voice. Suddenly, as if grown faint, he sank upon a chair and covered his eyes with his hands. Thus he remained for several moments, while his companions, awed by his emotion, waited in a silence not unmingled with curiosity. After awhile he took away his hand from his eyes and raised his face. Worn it was by the night's long ride and lack of food, sad it was, for he had but just come from the death-bed of a beloved parishioner, but above all it was glorified by a transfiguring faith.

"A little maid," he repeated, and now his voice was tender; "she sits in prison on her straw pallet, knitting, and the good God watches over her."

In that solemn silence which followed

his words, the room lost all semblance to the Governor's state bed-chamber. Its spacious walls faded and narrowed to a prison cell, wherein on her straw pallet, sat a little maiden knitting.

The silence was broken by a smothered sob. The faithful little friend, her face buried on Lord Christopher's broad breast, was weeping.

When at last on that kind breast her sobs were hushed, the minister spoke again and she raised her head that she might listen.

He told them how the night before, after his supper at the inn-house, he had retired to his room to study. But he was restless and could not compose his thought, and whatever he wrote was meaningless. So, believing this non-success to be a re-proof from the Lord, inasmuch as he was writing on a profane and worldly subject, he laid down his quill and fastened his papers with a weight, that the breeze coming in the open window might not blow them away. Then had he opened his Bible. Now the breeze was grateful to him, for his room was warm. A subtle fragrance of the meadow and the peace of the night seemed to be wafted about him. He was reminded how one of the Patriarchs of old had gone "forth into the fields at even-tide to pray." This thought was gracious and so won upon him, that he rose and snuffed his candles, and went out into a wide field lying back of the inn.

The moon was not risen, but the night was so fair and holy by reason of the starlight, that the white reflection of some young meadow birches showed in the stream, and, a distance off, he could see the moving shapes of some cows. He heard the tinkling of their bells. He felt no longer restless but at deep peace.

It seemed not long before he heard the night watchman making his rounds, crying all good folk in for the night. He heard him but faintly, however, as in a dream. His heart was exceedingly melted and he felt God in an inexpressible manner, so that he thought he should have fallen into a trance there in the meadow. The summons of the night watchman began to sound louder in his ears, so, reminding himself that the greatest duty was ever the nearest duty, he turned to go toward the inn-house. Just then he saw near the cluster of meadow birches, the little maid he had visited in prison in the afternoon. She was clothed in shining white and transparent in the starlight as a wan ghost.

Still, by the glory in her face, he knew it was not her Dead Shape, but her resurrected self. As he would have spoken she vanished, and only the white trunks of the young birches remained.

By this, he knew it was a sign from God that she was innocent, being showed to him as if caught up to Heaven. At this he remembered her words in prison, when Sir Jonathan had sought to make her confess by threatening that she should be put to death by stones.

An enraged groan and a missile thrown interrupted him. The pale student in his passion had hurled his wine-mug across the room.

" And you sat by and heard that vile

wretch so torture a child!" he cried. "Oh, my God! of what stuff are these thy ministers fashioned, that this godly servant of thine did not take such a living fiend by the scruff of his neck and fling him out of the cell?"

"Come, come, young sir," cried Sir William, angrily, "Mr. Mather had not then received the sign that your sister was not bound to the Evil One. I will have not the least discourtesy put upon him in my house, and the wine-mug flung in your wicked passion but just missed my head."

Cotton Mather waited patiently until the disturbance his words had wrought subsided. His ministerial experience had taught him sympathy with the humours of people in trouble. With a compassionate glance, directed toward the student, he continued to relate how he had straightway repaired to the inn, and ordering his horse saddled, had journeyed all night, that he might get a reprieve for the prisoner's life from Governor Phipps in time. He was delayed in seeing the Governor sooner, as upon entering Boston Town he was summoned to the death-bed of a parishioner.

"While all this but the more surely convinces me of the evil reality of this awful visitation of witches," he ended, "yet we must not put too much faith in pure spectre evidence, for it is proven in this case that the Devil did take upon himself the shape of one very innocent and virtuous maid."

"'Tis a very solemn question, my dear sir," rejoined the Cavalier, wagging his handsome head. "I remember once talking it over with my very honoured contemporary, Sir Thomas Browne. 'I am clearly of the opinion,' said he to me, 'that the fits are natural, but heightened by the Devil coöperating with the malices of the witches, at whose instance he does the villanies.'"

"Sir," asked Master Ronald of the Governor, "when will you give me the reprieve, that I may start at once for Salem?"

"Nay," cried Lord Christopher, "'twas I who brought trouble on the little maid. 'Tis I shall carry the reprieve."

"Methinks 'twere wisdom that I should go in person, accompanied by soldiers," spoke the Governor, "lest there be an uprising among the people at the reprieval of one convicted for witchery."

"Little mistress," said the Cavalier to Abigail, "be pretty-mannered and run and get me the decanter of wine from the living-room that we may again drink the health of the little maid in prison."

Abigail obediently went out into the hall. There she saw the pretty gentle-woman whom she had noticed in the garden, standing by the table, drawing off her gauntlet gloves. Behind her stood a little black Moor dressed in the livery of the Governor's household, and holding a basket filled with eggs and vegetables fresh from the market.

Lady Phipps turned as she heard steps behind her, and revealed a sprightly face with a fresh red colour, and fine eyes, black as sloes. "Lackaday, my pretty child!" she cried, "and prithee who might you be?"

Abigail dropped a courtesy. "I be

Abigail Brewster, of Salem Town," answered she.

"I hope I see you well," said the gentlewoman.

Abigail dropped another courtesy. "And it will pleasure you, madam," said she, "yon fine and portly gentleman, whom I come for to see, wishes more wine to drink therein the health of Deliverance Wentworth."

Lady Phipps shook her head. "I fear in drinking others' health he drinks away his own. I will attend to you in a moment, as soon as I have sent my little Moor to the kitchen with the marketing."

While Abigail waited there was a vigorous pounding in the adjoining room. At this, Lady Phipps smiled. "Our good guest be as hot tempered as hasty pudding be warm. Tell him, sweet child, that he must bide in patience a moment longer."

Abigail opened the door just wide enough to put her head inside. She saw Lord Christopher, purple in the face, frowning and tapping on the floor with his walking-stick. He smiled when he saw Abigail.

" Haste ye, little maid," he said blandly, " I wax impatient."

" Bide ye in patience, honoured sir," said Abigail, quoting the Governor's lady, and then she withdrew her head and shut the door.

Meanwhile Lady Phipps had dusted a lacquered tray which had been brought her from the East Indies, and laid upon it a square of linen. She cut some slices of pound cake, so rich that it crumbled, and laid them on a silver platter. She further placed some silver mugs and a plate of biscuit on the tray.

" Now you may take this in," she said, " and I will follow with the wine."

She crossed the hall and held the chamber-door open for the little maid to pass in. Perceiving the student inside, she bowed graciously, her fine black eyes twinkling.

Master Ronald put his hand to his heart and bowed very low, his cheek reddening, for he perceived by the twinkle in her eyes the drift of the madam's thought, — that she surmised him to be in trouble on account of some rude jesting.

Soon the door opened again and Lady Phipps entered with the wine, which she placed upon the table. She began to feel that this unusual gathering in her home, betokened more than some mere student prank, and her manner bespoke such a modest inquisitiveness, as they say in New England, that Lord Christopher, understanding, called her back as she was about to leave the room, and begged that she honour the poor tale he had to relate, by her gracious presence.

Chapter XVII

In a Sedan-chair

NEVER did Abigail forget that wonderful day. The journey could not be made until nightfall, as Lord Christopher, who insisted upon accompanying the expedition, would have to be bled and must rest during the afternoon. So Lady Phipps took the little maid with her, and changed the sad-coloured linsey-woolsey sacque and petticoat — having perceived a rent in the latter garment — for a white lute-string dress she herself had worn when young. Her own fair hands braided the little maid's soft brown hair and bound it with yellow ribbon, and she tied a similar ribbon around her waist. Abigail's shy brown eyes shone like stars and her cheeks were the colour of blush-roses.

Mr. Mather remained to dinner. Although solemn in some respects, it was on the whole a happy company that sat at the Governor's board that day.

After dinner Lady Phipps and Abigail went out into the garden, leaving the gentlemen to their pipes and conversation.

Lady Phipps mended the little petticoat with elaborate and careful darning. She told Abigail many stories and also had her little guest read aloud from the psalms. Thus the pleasant afternoon was whiled away. When at last the shadows began to lengthen in the pretty garden, and it was the hour of five by the ivy-festooned sun-dial, supper was served out of doors. The Governor and Master Ronald joined them. Mr. Mather had repaired to his home. Lord Christopher rested in his room. Then Lady Phipps hurried Abigail upstairs to don again her linsey-woolsey attire.

While thus engaged they heard a great trampling of horses.

" Oh, what may that be ?" cried Abigail, all agog.

" It is the soldiers who will accompany

my husband to Salem," replied her ladyship.

Abigail could scarce dress quickly
enough, so anxious was she to get downstairs. "And what may that other sound
o' laughing be?"

"It is made by the college students
outside," answered Lady Phipps, glancing out of the window; "they are seated
on the fence. They huzza because the
Governor is going to Salem to save your
friend. Lack-a-mercy-me! one great
bumpkin hath fallen backwards into my
flower-bed and broken the lily-stalks.
Off that fence they go, every mother's
son of them." And she flew out of the
room and ran downstairs while Abigail
hurried to the window.

She looked out upon a busy scene. It
was near sunset. The mellow light of
the departing day flashed upon the spear-
heads and muskets and the burnished
armour of mounted soldiers drawn up into
a group on the further side of the street.
Near by a Moor held two saddle-horses,
one of the steeds having a pillion. She

saw the students all tumble pellmell off the fence when Lady Phipps appeared, breathless with running, her fine black eyes flashing, as she lamented her lily-stalks. But the student who had fallen picked himself up and handed one of the broken stalks to her, with so much grace that she smiled and went back into the house.

Two black men now bore out the Governor's state sedan-chair, upholstered in crimson cloth and gold fringe, the outside painted cream-colour. It had one large glass door.

Lady Phipps hovered near, a feather duster in her hand.

Lord Christopher next appeared, leaning on two slaves, his face pale from his recent bleeding. Groaning, he seated himself in the chair. When he was comfortably settled, one of the slaves at her ladyship's direction shut the door.

Abigail saw Lord Christopher's face change from pallor to crimson.

He strove to open the door, but it was locked on the outside. He rapped sharply on the glass and shouted to the slave to let him out.

Lady Phipps, alarmed lest he have a fit or break the door, opened it herself.

"Madam," said the great physician, fixing her with his stern eye, "was it at your request that I was boxed up in this ungodly conveyance to suffocate to death?"

"Sir," replied she with spirit, "my glass door shall not go swinging loose to hit against the bearers' heels and be broken on the journey."

"Madam," thundered he, "am I to suffocate to gratify your inordinate vanities?"

Her ladyship tilted her chin in the air. "Sir," she replied, "nothing could compensate me for the breaking of that door."

"Madam," he retorted angrily, "in my condition, I should perish of the heat."

"Sir," she replied serenely, "I will lend you a fan."

His lordship gasped. The spectacle she invoked of himself sitting in a closed chair, energetically fanning himself through

Her ladyship tilted her chin
in the air

the long night, incensed him beyond the power of speech for several moments.

" Fy, fy, Lady Phipps," he said at last, wagging his head at her, " is this the way you Puritan wives are taught to honour your husbands' guests ? "

" Where should I find such another glass door ? " quoth she.

" Very well, madam," retorted he, " not one step do I go toward Salem, and that little maid may go hang, and her death will be due to your vanities and worldlinesses."

At this her ladyship's black eyes sparkled with wrath, but those near by saw her proud chin quiver, — a sign she was weakening.

For several moments there was silence. The students looked preternaturally grave. The waiting soldiers smiled. Lord Christopher folded his arms on his breast, rolled his eyes up to the ceiling of the chair, and sighed. The voices of Master Ronald and the Governor, inside the house, could be heard distinctly.

This painful calm was suddenly broken by a shrill little voice above their heads.

"Why don't ye take the door off'n its hinges and put it in the house?"

All looked up. There, leaning out of the second-story window, was a small excited maiden, unable to contain longer her anxiety at Lord Christopher's threat that her friend might go hang.

On beholding her, the students cheered, the soldiers laughed openly, and the slaves showed all their white teeth in delight.

"These Puritan children are wondrous blest with sense and wit," quoth Lord Christopher.

"Bring a wrench," ordered Lady Phipps. Thus the painful affair was happily solved.

Abigail, overcome at her temerity in calling out to the gentlefolk, drew away from the window and waited in much inquietude until she should be called.

Soon she heard Lady Phipps' voice at the foot of the stairs. "Hurry down, dear child; all are ready to start."

Outside, the Governor was mounted and waiting. Lord Christopher was drinking a glass of water, with a dash of rum in it as a tonic, preparatory to starting. Master Ronald had mounted the pillioned horse.

"Make haste, Mistress Abigail," he cried, "so we may be fairly on our way before nightfall." Old Pompey swung the little maid upon the pillion.

The Governor and the soldiers turned their horses' heads and rode off grandly. Next the four Moors lifted the handles of the sedan-chair, turned and followed. Master Ronald spurred his horse and it trotted off gayly.

Lady Phipps waved her lace-bordered kerchief and the Fellows of Harvard their caps. Abigail, sorry to say good-by, gazed backwards until her ladyship's lilac-gowned figure, surrounded by the students, with her kerchief fluttering, was hidden from sight by a turn of the road.

Little could Abigail foresee that within the course of several weeks, the dreaded accusation of witchcraft would be levelled at Lady Phipps.

Many townspeople stood agape on the road to see the imposing company go by and cross the Common, which was cool and green in the mellow light. The salt breeze was blowing off the sea. Early as it was, the gallants and their "Marmalet Madams" were strolling arm in arm. It was still light when the party reached the river. Here the ferryman took Lord Christopher across, the rest of the party taking the fordways a short distance above. As they entered the road on the other shore, Abigail was glad of companionship, so gloomily the forest rose on all sides. The night descended sultry and warm as if a storm were brewing. The moon had not yet risen, but a few pale stars shone mistily.

Now and then between the trees there flashed on their sight the white line of foam breaking along the beach of the ocean. They made their way tediously, those who rode suiting the gait of the horses to the rate of speed maintained by the chair-bearers. Often the poor fellows, straining under their heavy burden, stumbled on the rough road, jolting the invalid so that he swore mightily at them.

And there were many fordways to be crossed, so that he was carried up stream and down stream to find the most shallow places. Twice the streams were so swollen that the soldiers had to make rude bridges before Lord Christopher could be taken across.

Shortly before midnight, to the relief of all, the moon arose, breaking through light clouds.

Abigail first perceived it behind five tall pine trees.

"Master Ronald," she cried excitedly, "there be a witch's cottage back of those five pines."

"Nonsense," answered the student, glancing around him sharply.

"But I be sure o' it," averred Abigail. "I saw an old goody with a gobber tooth, cooking a witch-cake in a weamy-wimy hut, near five pine trees. And just beyond I drew her water in a bucket, at a spring."

Master Ronald, great as was his anxiety to press forward to Salem, nevertheless turned his horse's head and went up beyond the pines until he came to the spring. "Here is your spring, Mistress Abigail," he said, drawing rein and laughing with gay scorn; "come now, show me the old hag and her hut."

He looked back and saw the little maid's face white in the moonlight. "I ken not where it can be now," she said in a fearful whisper, "but it was there." She pointed to an empty space of ground where some flowers could be seen in the silver moonshine, but there was neither hut nor any sign of human habitation.

As the student observed these flowers a strange uneasiness took possession of him. A climbing rose stood upright in the air with naught to cling to, while the other flowers seemed to follow a pathway to an invisible dwelling.

"I beseech ye, let us hurry from the place," whispered Abigail, "it be uncanny. But there on that spot an hut stood when I went to Boston Town."

Master Ronald spurred his horse, but suddenly drew up again. "What was that?" he cried; "my horse stumbled."

"Hurry!" shrieked Abigail, glancing down and recognizing the outlines of the dark object, "it be the witch's pail."

Now Master Ronald, for all his fine scorn of witches, spurred his horse and rode on in a lively fashion. His face had grown so wet with perspiration that he was obliged to borrow Abigail's kerchief, his own not being convenient to get at under his belted doublet.

"It be the kerchief ye lent me this morn," said Abigail. She clasped her arms tightly around his waist, casting terror-stricken glances behind her. "Master Ronald," she inquired, recalling some of her father's tales, "ye don't see a wolf near by, do ye, with bloody jowls, a-sitting down, a-grinning at us?"

"I fear I am going in the wrong direction," he answered abstractedly; "we have gone some ways now. Your eyes are sharp, Mistress Abigail. See if you can distinguish our friends ahead."

"Not one do I see," she replied, after a moment's peering.

"We will turn back toward the sea," said the student, "and try to strike the path again from there."

Suddenly a lusty calling broke the silence.

"What can that be?" cried Master Ronald; "it sounds uncommon near."

"It be Lord Christopher's voice," said Abigail; "summat awful has happed."

"I cannot get the direction of the sound; can you?" asked the young man, holding his hand to his ear.

"Just ahead o' us," cried Abigail. "Hurry!"

After several moments of brisk riding they came to a bar of sand where the sea had once sent up an arm. All was silent again, save for the hooting of an owl.

"I see naught," said the student, reining in his horse.

"There below us be summat dark," said Abigail, pointing.

As she spoke, the calling for help broke forth again not a stone's throw from them.

This time the voice was unmistakably Lord Christopher's.

"Halloo!" cried Master Ronald, riding forward, "what's the matter there?"

"Don't come so near," came the reply, "there is quicksand. Lord have mercy on my soul!"

Master Ronald dismounted and ran toward Lord Christopher, relapsing into a cautious walk as he neared him.

"May Satan take the knaves that left me in this plight!" groaned his lordship.

And, although it was but a sorry time for laughter, Master Ronald, perceiving that his lordship was in no immediate danger, must needs clap his hands to his knees and double up with merriment. For while most of the chair rested on the solid earth, the back and one side tilted toward a strip of quicksand in such fashion that the invalid did not dare move, lest in his struggles to free himself, he tip the chair completely over and be swallowed up.

He smiled at Master Ronald's convulsed figure. "'Tis a merry jest, I wot, young sir," he said dryly, "but it so haps I be in no position to observe the marvellous humour of the situation."

"Sir," said Master Ronald, "I beg your pardon. Take a good grip of my hand. Now out with your best foot — the ground is solid here — wait till I brace myself. Ah-h-h!" and he tumbled over backwards, nearly pulling the invalid with him.

The chair, thus lightened, rose slightly from the quicksand. The young man seized the shafts and with a vigorous jerk had the chair on good, hard sand. But he pulled it over yet some way. "What became of the Moors, sir?" he asked.

Poor Lord Christopher leant heavily on the student's slender frame. "My lad," he said, "I wot not what I should have done had you not followed after. Those cowardly knaves, startled by a wolf crossing our path, dropped the shafts of my chair, and with a howl, fitter to issue from brutish throats than human, took to their heels without a thought of me."

"But what has become of the Governor?" asked the student.

"He and his soldiers had been a fair distance ahead of us, until my bearers, trying to find the smoothest path at my direction, lost their way," he answered, groaning.

"Bide you here," said the student, tenderly assisting him into his chair, "whilst I go and halloo to those rascals. They cannot be far off." Turning, he called to Abigail, "Be not afeared, Mistress Brewster, I will be back in a minute." And he ran on and vanished in the forest beyond.

The Cavalier and Abigail waited.

"My little maid," he called, breaking the silence between them, "come nearer."

Abigail crept over into the saddle and took the reins. "Get up," she said, shaking them. Her steed obediently stepped out into the strip of moonlit sand and she guided him over to the chair, the rich colouring of which in crimson and gold was to be faintly discerned.

"I have been thinking of my sweet

Elizabeth in Merry England," quoth his lordship.

"Ay," assented Abigail, listening intensely for any sound of the student; "ah, Master Ronald hath catched the knaves. I can hear their voices and the trampling of horses' feet."

"'Tis well," rejoined his lordship. "Little maid, I have been thinking of the words of my very learned contemporary, Sir Thomas Browne."

"And what might they be?" asked Abigail, giving him but half an ear.

"Great experience hath he had of death and hath seen many die," replied his lordship, solemnly, "for he too is a physician. Thus was he led to say that when he reflected upon the many doors which led to death, he thanked his God that he could die but once!"

Chapter XVIII

The Coming of Thomas

SOFTLY the daylight faded in Deliverance's prison-cell. But the purple twilight which brought repose after the day's work, and long hours of sweet sleep to the tired world, came sorrowfully to her anxious heart. Slowly, as the golden light which had filtered through the leaves of the apple tree was withdrawn, so moment by moment, hope vanished, and despair, like a pall of darkness, settled upon her.

The long day of patient waiting was past. No longer might her straining ears listen for Abigail's voice, for the tramp of horses' feet coming to her rescue from Boston Town, or, joy of joys, Ronald, Ronald, to clasp her in his arms and defy any to touch her harmfully.

All that day, at every step in the corridor, she had started and quivered, waiting with nerves strung to the highest tension. Now she knew the sun had set upon Abigail's failure.

The little maid had departed the morning of the previous day, and had she met with success, would have reached Boston Town in the evening, and have returned the next day to Salem.

Perhaps she had not been able to find the Cavalier, or had not found him soon enough and would arrive too late, or — and at this last thought, she shuddered — who could tell but that Abigail had mistaken her way and fallen a victim to the Indians or wolves, or a witch had cast a malignant spell upon her and she was wasting away in the forest, with none to know of her dire distress and to succour her. "Oh, Abigail," she whispered, " I wish ye had not gone ! I should have kenned better, for I be older than ye. Oh, Abigail ! I shall be hanged and not ken whether good or evil happed to ye. I was fair selfish to send ye."

With full and penitent heart, she

prayed that, although the Lord in His wisdom suffered her to die, yet he would, out of his great mercy, send her a sign that her sins had been forgiven, and her selfishness had not brought harm to Abigail.

Having thus prayed, she rose from her knees and sat down on the straw bed. The minutes passed. She heard the jailer open her door and put her supper on the floor, but she paid no heed to him. Time dragged by, and her cell was filled with gloom. The leaves at the window, however, were still brightly green in the outside light.

Yet God had sent no sign to her. She folded her hands patiently in her lap. "It will come," she murmured, with trustful eyes uplifted, "it will come."

In Prison Lane she heard a mad barking of dogs and the shouting of boys, directly under her window. The excited clamour died away in a few moments. Suddenly her attention was aroused by a plaintive crying. She glanced up. Looking at her through the bars on the outside window-ledge, was a limp, bedraggled and forlorn kitten with a torn ear. It had climbed the apple tree to be rid of its merciless pursuers.

Deliverance jumped to her feet and stretched forth her arms with a cry of joy.

"Oh, Thomas, Thomas, the Lord hath sent ye as a sign to comfort me!"

The kitten mewed sympathetically. It made its way in through the bars to the inner ledge. Then it thrust a shrinking paw downwards, but hastily drew it back. Deliverance was puzzled to know how to reach the little creature.

She held up her petticoat like a basket and coaxed the kitten to jump, but without effect. Then she made a shelf of her hands, held high as possible, while she stood on tip-toes. But the shaking hands offered no safety to the shrinking kitten.

Yet the tender, beseeching tones of his little mistress won at last upon the cowardly soul of Thomas and fired him to dare all. He made an unexpected flying leap, landing on the golden head as the securest foothold. There he slipped and scrambled valiantly, until two eager hands lifted him down and the beloved little voice, broken with sobs, cried, "Oh, Thomas, my own dear Thomas, the Lord has sent ye as a sign to comfort me!"

Thus Thomas, a starved, runaway kitten, worn to a shadow, chased by dogs, ready to die of exhaustion, came into his own again.

Deliverance learned a lesson that evening which all must learn, sooner or later, that the crust thankfully shared with another, makes even prison-fare sweeter and more satisfying than plenty served in luxury and loneliness.

The corn mush and milk, which at times she had refused with a disdainful toss of her little head, now became a delicious dish with a rare savour, such as she had never before perceived. For while she ate from one side of the bowl with a spoon, Thomas, on the opposite side, drank the milk with incessant lapping of his small pink tongue, until in his eagerness to drain it, he thrust his two front feet in the bowl.

"Thomas, ye unmannerly person," cried Deliverance, "what would ye think o' me to be putting my two feet in the bowl?" And she lifted him up and went back to her straw bed, while Thomas, loudly purring, curled up in slumber in her lap.

The cell had now grown so dark that a flash of orange-light showing in the crack beneath the door, startled her, reminding her that the jailer was making his nightly rounds. Alarmed lest the kitten should be discovered, she pushed it under the straw. She was none too soon, for in another moment the door was flung open and revealed the jailer with his lantern, which made a circle of yellow light around him and showed the feet of another person following.

This personage was none other than Sir Jonathan Jamieson. The light shone on the tip of his long nose, his ruddy beard, the white ruff above his sable cape. As he was about to cross the threshold, he started and drew back. The jailer also started and his knees knocked together.

"Methought I heard a strange noise," said Sir Jonathan with dignity. "I will investigate."

The jailer clutched his cape. "My lord, my lord, meddle with no witch, lest ye tempt the Devil."

Again they heard the strange sound. The lantern's circle of light fell half-way across the floor of the cell. Beyond, and concealed by the shadow, Deliverance, terror-stricken, held the outraged Thomas firmly under the straw.

"It sounds like a cat," quaked the jailer, and he straightway forgot all his previous doubts as to the guilt of the prisoner. "The witch be turning herself into an imp o' Satan."

While Sir Jonathan still hesitated, there came a long-drawn-out, blood-curdling cry. Bravely, he raised his walking-stick and tapped stoutly on the floor. "Scat!" he cried in a voice that shook slightly, "scat!"

"Miow," answered the angry Thomas.

Shudderingly, the jailer reached in past Sir Jonathan, pulled the door to and locked it. Then, grown too weak to hold the lantern, he set it on the floor, and leant against the wall, his knees knocking together even more violently than before. "Oh, miserable doubter that I ha' been!" he chattered, "'t be a judgment come upon me."

Sir Jonathan leant against the wall on the opposite side of the corridor, with his knees shaking also. "Since it troubles you, goodman," he said, "I shall not persist in entering, although I cling to the opinion that when one is sufficient exalted in spiritual things, the Devil has no power over him."

"I ha' been a miserable doubter," chattered the jailer; "the Lord ha' mercy on my soul!"

From the cell came again that terrible cry, a wailing, mournful sound, so wild and eerie as to strike terror to stouter hearts.

"The witch be calling on her Master, Satan," chattered the jailer.

"Ay, pray," muttered Sir Jonathan; "you must have an ill conscience, goodman, to be so afeared. But let me haste away; the time waxes apace and the night watchman will be making his rounds."

Perhaps it was part of his punishment that from that hour Sir Jonathan was never free from dread. He, who originally had no faith in witchcraft and secretly laughed at it, although he falsely testified to his belief in it, was doomed, henceforth, to start at his own shadow, to cower in bed, to ever after keep a night-light burning. He hurried along in the silver moonlight which fell whitely on the pebbled street, a solitary black figure with flapping cape and steeple-hat.

Suddenly, he drew back with a shrill cry, startled by his own shadow flung ahead of him as he turned a corner. So, cowering and starting, he reached his room and crept into his bed, there to fall into an uneasy slumber, which the taper's pale flame was as ineffectual to calm as the light of truth to reach his darkened heart.

Meanwhile, an indignant kitten stood gasping and sneezing, nearly choked by the straw under which it had lain.

Ah! how its little mistress held it to

her breast and soothed it and kissed it, weeping for thanksgiving that she had been spared a visit from Sir Jonathan. There were hours, however, in the long unhappy night, when not even the kitten nestled in her arms could comfort Deliverance, — hours when all the bright days of her life came trooping through her fancy, to be realized no more.

Never again would she be filled with joy that the fruit trees blew sweet in blossom, that the violets budded in the long grass in the orchard, that she and Abigail had found a bird's nest holding four blue eggs, or had happened upon a patch of strawberries. There were other times which would not return, — the moonlit winter nights, fairer than the days, when she and Goodwife Higgins went to husking-bees and quilting parties. Not for her would there be a red ear found amidst the corn. Still sadder were her thoughts of her father, missing her help with the herbs, blundering in his helpless fashion over the task that had once been hers.

Goodwife Higgins would have no one

left now to mind her of the little daughter that had died so long ago of the smallpox.

And there was one other whom she had not seen for many months.

"Oh, Ronald!" she whispered, "my heart be full o' grief that ye could not come to me."

After a weary while she fell into a deep sleep from which she was wakened by the jailer.

For the first time he spoke to her harshly, roughly bidding her rise and prepare for death.   He pushed the bowl containing her breakfast inside the threshold with his foot, fearing to enter the cell.   So hurried was his glance that it failed to take in Thomas, snuggled up warmly in the depression in the straw, made where Deliverance had slept.

Sadly the little maid dressed herself and braided her hair.

She ate a little of the mush and milk, but she fed most of it to Thomas.

"Thomas," she said, tipping the bowl conveniently for him, "my own dear Thomas, I hope ye will not forget me.

Ye can go home again, Thomas, but I shall never see my home again."

After this she rose and put the cell in order, making the straw bed over nicely. Then she wrote a note on a leaf torn from Abigail's diary, and pinned this note by a knitting-needle on the stocking she had completed. Having finished, she sat down and waited patiently. It was not long before the jailer again appeared. She saw behind him the portly Beadle.

" How now, witch," cried the latter, peering in over the old man's shoulder, " hath prison-fare fattened ye?"   But as he caught sight of the prisoner he started. " I' faith," he cried, " how peaked ye be. Go in, goody, and fetch her forth," he commanded the jailer.

" Na step will I take toward the witch," chattered the jailer.

" Step in, step in, goody," advised the Beadle; " how can I convey the witch away unless ye free her?"

But the jailer was not to be persuaded to go near the prisoner. He and the Beadle fell into an angry controversy over the matter and were near to serious quarrelling, when a soldier appeared at the doorway.

"What causeth the delay?" cried the guard, crossly. "Hath the witch flown out of the window?"

"They be feared lest I cast a spell on them and so dare not unlock my chain," spoke Deliverance, "but I wot not how to cast a spell and I would, good sir."

"Give me the keys," said the guard, brusquely. He snatched them in no gentle manner from the jailer. "Enough, enough of this foolishness, ye chicken-hearted knaves. Stand up, mistress," he added, entering the cell.

He knelt in front of the little maid, fumbling to find the right key of the bunch. Deliverance, suddenly grown faint, rested one hand on his shoulder. He started and his heart leapt for fear, but the continued touch of the small, trembling hand, so weak and helpless, changed his fear to pity. So he said naught, but was willing the witch-maid should lean on his strong shoulder. He unlocked the padlock and flung the chain aside. Deliverance stood unbound once more.

She turned and lifted the stocking with the note pinned on it, from the floor.

"Oh! would ye mind," said she, "to bear this to my father for me?"

The soldier, with a gruff assent, put the stocking and note in his pocket. He turned away, no longer caring to look into those blue, beseeching eyes, which filled him with tormenting misgivings.

"Come, come," he cried to the Beadle, "it waxeth past time. Let an ill duty be done quickly, say I." He strode out of the cell and down the corridor.

The Beadle reached in and touched Deliverance's shoulder with his staff of office. "Step forth," he commanded, "and follow yon soldier, and I will come up behind."

Suddenly the little maid bent down and lifted something from the straw pallet. As she turned they saw she held a little black kitten, curled in slumber, against her breast.

The old jailer shuddered and muttered a prayer, and the Beadle's fat face grew white. They believed that she, after the manner of witches, had summoned an imp from Hell to bear her company.

Close to the prison door was drawn a rude cart, with a stool fastened to the floor in the back. The driver, indifferent through much similar experience, sat nodding on the seat. The soldier who had preceded Deliverance, waited to assist her in the cart, which was too high a step for a little maid. He lifted her in bodily, kitten and all, keeping his eyes turned from her face.

The driver clucked to his horse, the soldier mounted his and rode ahead, and the Beadle walked pompously at the side of the cart, moving slowly down the street.

All Salem had gathered to behold this hanging, which was of awful import to the townspeople, brought to a frantic belief that Satan had taken possession of the heart of one of their children, known and loved by them all her life. A strange, sad thing it was that the Devil should have taken on himself the guise of a motherless young maiden.

So although the crowd through which the cart passed was large, but little noisy demonstration was made, and few curses or mutterings heard. Several boys who ventured to call jeeringly, were sternly hushed. In the throng there was only one near friend to the prisoner. This was Goodwife Higgins, who plodded bare-headed beside the cart, weeping. Neither her father nor brother was to be seen. All night following the trial, Master Wentworth had wandered in the fields in a drenching rain, and had returned home to succumb to an illness, from which he daily grew weaker, lying unconscious this very morning.

Many of the women were affected to tears by the sight of the little maid, seated on the stool in the cart, the kitten clasped to her breast.

Deliverance knew naught of this sym-pathy. She had but a dull sense of many people, and that the sun had never shone so brightly before. She was dazed by terror and grief, and a stupor crept over her, so that her head hung heavily on her breast and her limbs seemed cold and of leaden weight.

The cart passed out of the street into a rocky path, and ascended by imperceptible degrees to the summit of a low, green hill.

The little maid lifted her head and looked steadfastly at the scaffold there erected. On the platform she saw the figures of the minister and the hangman, dark against the blue sky.

u

On Gallows' Hill

AT the foot of this scaffold, the driver stopped. Deliverance was bidden to step out. Attended by the guard, she ascended the ladder. Only one instinct remained to the heartbroken child, and that was to clasp still closer to her breast the little kitten, the one faithful and loving friend who clung to her in this dread hour.

"Deliverance Wentworth," spoke the minister in a loud, clear voice, "will you, while there is yet time, confess your sin of witchery, or will you be launched into eternity to the loss of your immortal soul?"

She looked at him vaguely. His words had not pierced to her dulled comprehension.

He repeated them.

Again she was silent. Slowly her unresponsive gaze turned from the minister and swept the sea of upturned faces. Never was there a sterner, sadder crowd than the one upon which she looked down; the men lean, sour-visaged, the women already showing a delicacy, born of hardship and the pitiless New England winters. Children hoisted on the shoulders of yeomen were to be seen. She saw the wan, large-eyed face of little Ebenezer Gibbs, as his father held him up to behold the witch who had afflicted him with such grievous illness. Drawn together in a group were the gentry. And all thrilled to a general terror for none knew on whom the accusation might next fall. At the tavern, the loiterers, made reckless by the awful plague, gathered to be merry and pledge a cup to the dying.

With these latter mingled foreign sailors, their faces bronzed, wearing gold rings in their ears and gay scarves around their waists.

One of these tavern roisterers shouted: " Behold the imp the witch carries in the shape of a black cat !"

There came another cry : " Let the cat be strung up also, lest the witch's spirit pass into it at her death !"

Others caught up and repeated the cry. An ominous murmur rose from the crowd, drowning the single voices.

The minister strove in vain to make himself heard.

To Deliverance the clamour was meaningless sound. But yet closer to her breast she clasped the little kitten.

Slowly she turned her head and her gaze travelled over the landscape. Vaguely she felt that she would never see the morrow's sun, that now she looked her last upon the kind earth.

Suddenly her gaze became fixed as she caught the flash of spears and saw mounted soldiers emerge from the forest and come rapidly down the winding road from the opposite hill. Some dim instinct of self-preservation struggled through the stupor which enveloped her. She raised her arm and pointed to the forest. So strange, so silent, seeming guided by a mysterious power, was that gesture, that a tremor as at something supernatural passed through the people.

They saw the minister speak excitedly to the hangman, whose jaw dropped in amazement. Soon was distinctly heard the trampling of horses. A moment later four soldiers, riding two abreast, swept up the hill with cries of: —

"Way, make way, good people, in the King's name!"

Following these came his Excellency the new Governor, Sir William Phipps. He sat severely erect on his richly caparisoned horse, attended by two more soldiers. Reaching the scaffold he reined in his horse and waited. A yet more astonishing thing than the unlooked-for arrival of the Governor was about to occur.

There next appeared, a goodly distance behind, a sedan-chair carried by four Moors. The occupant of the chair was a man of great size, whose left leg was bandaged and rested on a pillow. Despite the cool morning the sweat was rolling off his face, and he groaned. But dusty, warm, and in pain as he seemed, he had a most comely countenance. The silken chestnut curls fell on his shoulders, whilst his high and haughty nose bespoke power in just proportion to the benevolence of his broad brow. As the slaves bore him along very slowly, for they were much exhausted, Sir Jonathan Jamieson, making his way through the crowd to join a group of the gentry, crossed the path directly in front of the sedan-chair. Here he paused, lingering a moment, to get a glimpse of the Governor, not turning his head to perceive what was behind him.

As he thus paused, the stranger was observed to half rise and draw his sword. But suddenly his face changed colour, his sword arm fell, and he sank back on his pillows, his hand clutching his side. Those near by heard him murmur, " As Thou hast forgiven me, even me." But the rest of the way to the scaffold not once did he raise his head nor remove his hand from his side.

Sir Jonathan passed serenely, swinging

his blackthorn stick, all unwitting how nigh death he had been in that short moment.

Next there came riding a-horseback, Master Ronald Wentworth, the brother of the condemned maid.

His student's cap was set on the back of his head, his dark locks falling on either side of his white face, his small-clothes and riding boots a-colour with the mud.

But doubtless the most astonishing sight of all to the amazed people was a small, mud-bespattered maiden, attired in sad-coloured linsey-woolsey, seated on a pillion behind the Fellow of Harvard, her chin elevated in the air, her accustomed meekness gone.

This important personage was the missing Abigail Brewster.

When these last arrivals had reached the scaffold, Governor Phipps dismounted, and giving his horse into the care of a soldier ascended the ladder to the platform. His face was pale and his expression ill-favoured, as if he relished not the discomfort he had undergone. The murmurings and whispers had died down.   His words were anxiously attended.

"My good people," he commenced solemnly, "it hath become my duty to declare unto you that I came, not to pardon Deliverance Wentworth, but to declare her innocent of the charge brought against her, for the which she has been condemned to death.   Circumstances have been so cunningly interwoven by the Evil One as to put upon this young maid, whom I pronounce wholly free and innocent of blame, the character of a witch.   Lord Christopher Mallett, Physician to his Majesty the King, hath matter whereof he would speak to you to warn you of the evils attaching to an o'er hasty judgment.

"But there is yet another word, which I, your Governor, would impress with all solemnity upon you.   Assisted by that godly minister, Master Cotton Mather, I have made careful study of the will of the Lord regarding the sin and punishment of witchery.   Better, far better, I say unto you, that twenty innocent people should be made to suffer than that one witch should go unhanged when you have catched her. This I say because we are now in a fair way to clear the land of witches. I would have you abate not one jot nor tittle of the zeal you have so far manifested, lest the good work be half done and thereby nothing be accomplished. For but one witch left in the land is able to accomplish untold evil. Therefore, while the Lord hath been gracious to so expediently correct the error of your judgment in sentencing this maid to be hanged, yet I do not condemn your error, but see rather, within the shell of wrong, the sweet kernel of virtuous intent, that you spared not in your obedience to the Lord's behest, one who, by reason of her tender years, appealed most artfully to your protection."

Thereat the Governor ceased speaking, and seated himself on a stool which had been carried up on the scaffold for him.

Eagerly the people speculated as to the cause of this unlooked-for pardon. As the Governor ceased speaking, the tavern roisterers sent up shouts and tossed off mugs of sack. One fellow, a merry-andrew of the town, turned handsprings down the road. This uncouth and ill-timed merriment was speedily checked by the authorities.

Meanwhile the Beadle was seen to go up and place a stool on the scaffold. Then he went half-way down the ladder and took a pillow and another stool handed up to him, and arranged these in front of the first seat, after which he descended, for the platform was not strong, and already accommodated three people besides Deliverance : the Governor, the minister, and the hangman.

Now the ladder bent and creaked under a tremendous weight, as Lord Christopher Mallett, panting for breath, pausing for groans at every step, ascended by painful degrees and dropped so heavily upon the stool placed in readiness for him that the frail structure shook dangerously. Assisted by the hangman, he lifted his gouty leg on the pillowed stool. Then he saw Deliverance standing near by, and stretched forth his hands, while a smile lighted with its old-time geniality his worn countenance.

"Come hither, little mistress," he said, "and let me feast my eyes on you, for I swear no more doughty and brave-hearted lass abides in his Majesty's kingdom."

But Deliverance stood still, regarding him with dull eyes. Something in the delicate child-mind had been strained beyond endurance.

The black kitten struggled from her arms and leapt to the floor of the platform, craning its head with shrinking curiosity over the edge.

Slowly, something familiar in the kindly face and the outstretched hands of the great physician made itself apparent to Deliverance's benumbed faculties. Troubled, she looked long at him. Over her face broke a sweet light, the while she plucked daintily at her linsey-woolsey petticoat. "Ye can feel for yourself, good sir, and ye like," she said in her sweet, high treble, "that it be all silk without'n a thread o' cotton in it."

As she spoke she drew nearer him, but before she reached him, put out her arms with a little fluttering cry and sank at the great physician's feet.

When consciousness returned to her, she found herself seated on some gentleman's lap. Her temples were wet with a powerful liquid whose reviving odour she inhaled. Not then did she realize that she was indeed seated on the lap of that austere dignitary, Governor Phipps. At perfect peace she sat with her golden head resting against his purple velvet coat, her eyelids closed from weariness, her confusion gone. Dimly as in a dream she heard the voice of Lord Christopher addressing the people.

"In this town of Salem, I had reason to believe, resided one who had recently come as a stranger among you. This stranger to you, had been my cherished friend, my confidant in all things, and he betrayed me. Traitor though he was, I could have forgiven him, perceiving now with clearer eyes his weakness against a great temptation, but he hath shamefully persecuted a child, which, of all sins, is the most grievous."

The speaker paused and his piercing glance singled out one of the group of gentry, gathered on the edge of the crowd.   The man thus marked by that gaze was Sir Jonathan Jamieson.   A moment he returned that challenging, scornful look; then as the eyes of all near by turned toward him, his face whitened and, with a defiant raising of his head, he turned abruptly and strove to make his way out of the crowd.

"Let me pass, churls," he cried fiercely, glancing round, " or I will crack your pates."

So those who stood by, being yeomen, and naturally awed by those of gentle blood, drew aside at the threat, albeit they muttered and cast dark looks upon Sir Jonathan as he passed.

This scene was observed by very few, as the great body of people hung intent upon Lord Christopher's words.

" This man," he continued, "was, as I told you, my cherished friend, my confidant in all things, although he possessed no interest in my craft.   Being of a book-ish turn of mind, he treated with friendly derision and apparent unconcern my experiments in leechcraft and chirurgery, professing no faith in them.   Now it having been my practice to consult regularly a soothsayer, I learned from him that in two years' time England would be visited by the Black Plague.   Thereby I was greatly saddened and sorrowed o' nights, having visions of good folk dying in the streets and carted off to the potter's field.   Most of all did I think of the poor children who have not their elders' philosophy to bear pain and are most tender to suffer so.   The thought of these poor little ones so worked upon me that I had no peace.   At last an idea of great magnitude took possession of me.   In the two years' time that was to elapse afore this terrible visitation would take place, I resolved to discover a simple which would be both a preventive and a cure for this plague with which the Lord sees fit to visit us at sundry times.   I took his Majesty the King into my confidence. The proposed adventure received his gracious approval. For its furtherance he gave me large monies, and I also used the greater substance of my house. I travelled to India to consult with Eastern scholars, wondrously learned in mysterious ways beyond our ken. Weeks, day and night, I spent in experimenting. At last one morn, just as the day broke, and its light fell on my two trusty servitors who had fallen asleep e'en as they stood assisting me, I gave a great shout for joy. My last experiment had stood the test. I had triumphed. The recipe was perfected. 'Wake, wake,' I cried, 'and give thanks unto God.'

"So powerful was the powder, of such noble strength, that e'en its odour caused my daughter to swoon lily-white when I would have administered a dose to her as a preventive against sickness in the future. One man only besides the King was in my confidence. This was my friend and he was my undoing. Whilst I was in attendance upon his Majesty who had been wounded at a boar-hunt, this false friend, having free access to my house, entered and stole the parchment having the recipe.   With a wounded heart I set to work again to recall the intricate formula of the recipe.   I was unsuccessful.   Papers of value leading to the composing of the cure were left me, but the amount and proper compounding of the ingredients had been set down only in the stolen parchment.   To add to my trouble I perceived that the King's faith in me was shaken, that he regretted the monies put at my disposal.   Moreover, he credited not my tale of my false friend's baseness, but professed to think I had failed, and strove to hide my discomfiture beneath a cloak of lies.   I despaired.   At last I learned that my enemy had gone to America and landed at ye Town of Boston, whither I followed him.   I arrived after a favourable voyage and sought your Governor.   To him alone I gave my rightful name and mission.   And here with much secrecy I was obliged to work, having no proof by which to confirm my accusation.

My only hope lay in surprising my enemy afore he had time to destroy the parchment from fear and malice. My search led me to your town. It was the close of day. I sent my Indian guide to a farmhouse for food, and seated myself on a fallen tree for a resting-minute. I was o'er cautious and determined not to enter the town afore nightfall, desiring that my enemy should not recognize me, if I by any inadvertence happed to cross his path. As I waited, there came tripping along this same little maid whom you would have hanged.

"I learned from her of the stranger in your town. Thereat I resolved to go back to Boston Town and obtain assistance to arrest this base traitor. Now, prompted by an unfortunate desire to annoy him and full of triumph, I did whisper in the little maid's ear tormenting words to say when next she met him, chuckling to myself as I thought of his astonishment that a fair and innocent child should have an inkling of his guilt. So high did my spirits rise after the little maid left me that I could not sit still, but must needs rise

and stroll down the path to meet my Indian
guide.   There I met an old silly, praying.
I dropped a black pellet in one of his pails
of milk as an idle jest.   But I have paid
dearly for my malicious chuckling.   I have
paid well."   The speaker paused to groan
and wipe the sweat from his brow.

"I have travelled far in uncivilized
countries, amidst savage people," he continued, "but ne'er have I known such a
terrible journey as I endured last night.
The memory of it will last me throughout
this world, and who knows and the Lord
forgive not my sins, but that I shall remember it in the next.   I was carried up
stream and down stream, terrible insects
arose with a buzzing sound and fastened
themselves on my flesh, the howling of
wild beasts smote my ears.   Yet am I
thankful to have made that journey, for
by it I have saved the life of a brave lass
who hath done a doughtier deed in her
King's service than any of you who have
prosecuted her.   It was her nimble wit,
working in prison, that obtained the stolen
parchment and sent it to me.   Through

her messenger I learned of my enemy's intent to strike at my very vitals, my high position and favour with the King. He was having the recipe compounded, to return with it to England and obtain the honour of its discovery himself. But thanks be to God, the evil of his ways was his undoing. This little maid whom you would have hanged hath saved England from the plague, and I am made her debtor for life."

A shout broke from the stern, repressed Puritans.

" Let us behold the little maid who hath saved England. Let the child stand forth."

Governor Phipps put Deliverance upon her feet, and holding her hand walked to the edge of the platform. When the people saw her in her sad-coloured gown, her hair a golden glory around her face, they were silent from awe and self-reproach. Only when the kitten leapt upon her petticoat and climbed to her shoulder, there seating itself with rightful pride, the sober Puritans broke into wild shoutings and laughter. Laughter mingled with tears, that in all the town of Salem, so brave a maid had found in her extremity but two loyal friends, Mistress Abigail Brewster and a little kitten.

Deliverance, frightened by the cries and unwonted animation of the upturned faces, began to weep and put out her arms pitifully to Lord Christopher.

"Oh, might it pleasure ye to take me home, good sir?"

Before he could reply, a young man bounded up the ladder and caught the little maid in his arms.

"I could keep from you no longer, sweetheart," he cried.

Deliverance's arms tightened around his neck. "I be o'er glad to see ye, dear Ronald," she said, laying her head on his shoulder, "and, oh, let it pleasure ye not to dilly-dally, but to take me to father, for I be fair weary to see him?"

So the Fellow of Harvard, with a word to his Excellency for permission, slowly descended the ladder with his precious burden in his arms.

Thus Deliverance returned to her father.

Chapter XX

The Great Physician

WHEN the excitement had subsided somewhat, Lord Christopher was seen to lean forward with renewed earnestness, raising his hand impressively.

"My dear people," he said, and the great physician's voice was tender as if speaking to sick and fretful children, "my dear people, God hath afflicted you more sorely with this plague of witchery than with the Black Plague itself. Yet it lies with you to check this foul disease. The Bible says, 'Thou shalt not suffer a witch to live.' But it also commands, 'Judge not, that ye be not judged.' Abide by the latter injunction, that you save your souls from sin and let not your land run red with innocent blood. Let each one of you be so exalted in goodness that evil cannot enter into you. But,

and my words on witchery impress you
not, let me at least beseech you who are
of man's estate and have catched a child
in sin, to remember that it but does as
those around it, and is therefore to be
dealt by tenderly.

"And yet another subject am I driven
to speak to you upon.

"Mightily does it distress me that you
do bring your children up in woeful ignorance of the Christmas-tide as we celebrate
it in Merry England. 'Tis very dolorous
that you should be so blinded as to think
the proper observance of that Holy day
bewrayeth a Popish tendency. Methinks
it be a lack of good red blood that makes
you all so sour and mealy-mouthed. Your
Governor informs me that on that blessed
day, sadly you wend your way to church,
with downcast eyes as though you were
sinners catched in naughtiness. There is
great droning of psalms through your
noses, which is in itself a sorry thing, and
I doubt not, an unpleasant sound in the
Lord's ear. Whereas, in green old England, the little children carol all day long.

But here not even your babes have sugar-plums. My stomach turns against you and your ways. How different is it in my castle across the seas! To the mantel above the blazing yule-log, my sweetest daughter pins her stocking. Outside, the snow snaps with the cold and the frost flowers whiten the window-pane. Then come the village lads and lassies singing, that we may open the window and fling out siller pieces, sometimes a bit of bright gold.

" Lastly, at the chiming of the midnight bells, troop in my servant-men and wenches. One and all we drink the hot-spiced glee-wine my sweet Elizabeth makes in the silver wassail bowl. And to every man and maid I give a piece of gold.

" I do beseech you, good people, to have remembrance after this, that Christmas is children's day, and that to keep it with sadness and dolour, is an offence unto the Lord Christ, whose birth made that day, and who was said by those versed in wisdom, to have been when a child tender,

holy, and gay, as it becometh all children
to be. Therefore I would have you be-
stow these delights upon your children,
for they are bowed by responsibilities
beyond their years, and joy is checked in
them, so that I oft catch myself sighing,
for I have great pain not to see all children joyful and full of the vigour of life.

"Thus I would make an example of the
little maid whom you have persecuted,
that you may deal gently with children, remembering how near you were to shedding
her innocent blood. I beseech you, by
the grievous sin that you and your learned
judges so nearly committed, to be tender
with the poor children, knowing they
speak the truth, unless you do so fright
them that in bewilderment they seek to
save themselves by a falsehood and know
not into what evil they fall thereby. When
you are tempted to severity, inquire well
into the merits of the case, lest you do an
injustice, keeping in mind the persecution
of the little maid who hath saved England."

Thus Lord Christopher ceased speaking.

In the years to come it was related that his speech was so affecting as to draw tears to the eyes of all, and that many a parent in Salem was known thereafter to refrain from harsh reproof of a child, because of the great physician's words and the love that all learned to bear him during the weeks his illness forced him to remain in Salem.

Regarding his earnest request that Christmas be observed by them after his irreverend fashion, they did not condemn him for his Popish tendency, but winked at it, as it were, knowing he had other virtues to counterbalance this weakness. Being altogether charmed by him, they earnestly trusted that for his own good he might come round to their way of thinking.

During those few weeks his presence shed the only brightness in the panic-stricken town. While he was powerless to avert the awful condition, there were nevertheless many sad hearts which were made lighter, merely to visit him in his sick-room at the tavern. And the goodwives, finding their dainties did not please him as much as the sight of their little children, ceased not to send the former, but instead sent both.

When at last he was able to leave his room, Lord Christopher went one afternoon to Deliverance's home.

Gladly he entered the forest road, thankful to leave the town behind him. The terrible trials still continued. Only that morning he had seen two persons hanged, and there was a rumour that a ship infected with smallpox had entered the harbour.

He walked slowly, leaning on his stick, for he was yet very lame. The greenness and peace of the majestic forest were grateful to him. Soon he came in sight of Master Wentworth's home. In the open doorway he saw Deliverance seated at her spinning-wheel, singing as she guided the thread.

Already the roses bloomed again in the little maid's face, and never was heart so free from sorrow as hers, save for that touch of yearning which came to her whenever her glance rested on her father, who, since his illness, was gentler and quieter than ever, seldom entering the still-room, and devoting many hours to sitting on the stoop, dreaming in the sunshine.

Master Ronald had not yet returned to Boston Town, loath to leave his little sister, still fearful for her safety, not knowing in which direction the wind of public opinion might veer.

Glancing up from his book this afternoon, as he lay on the grass, under the shade of a tree, he saw Lord Christopher approaching. So he rose quickly, and went down to the gate to greet the great physician.

And the two, Lord Christopher leaning heavily on the student's arm, for he was wearied by his walk, went up the path to where little Deliverance sat spinning.

Lord Christopher had a long talk with Master Wentworth this afternoon and at the end of their conversation, the latter called his children to him.

" Ronald," he said, " and you, my little Deliverance, Lord Christopher urges me to return to England where he promises me, my lad, that you shall have all advantage in the way of scholarly pursuits, and that you, Deliverance, shall be brought up to be his daughter's companion. What say you both? The question is one which you must decide. I," he added sadly, yet with a wondrous sweetness in his face, "will not abide many years longer with you; and my future is not in England, but in a fairer land, and the sea I must cross greater than the one you know, so I would fain leave you with a protector in this harsh world."

A long silence followed his words. Then Ronald spoke. "Sir, I have none other wish than to continue in this country in which I was born and which has ever been my home. Surely I know the constant toil, the perils from savages and wild beasts, the stern laws we Puritans have made for each little sin, alas! the hardships too often known, and the gloom of our serious thought which o'ershadows all. Yet through this sombre sky, the sun will shine at last as brightly as it shines in

England. In the University that has nourished in me patriotism and liberty of thought, I have grown to believe that here in this wilderness is the basis for a greater England than the England across the seas."

The student's face glowed with ardour, his eyes were brilliant as if he saw visions the others comprehended not.

"And you, Deliverance," asked her father, tenderly.

Now the little maid's fancy had woven a picture of herself in a court dress of crimson velvet, her hair worn high, a lace collar falling on her shoulders, a rose in her hand such as was carried by the little court lady of the miniature. But her imagination, which had soared so high, sank at Ronald's words.

"What say you, little mistress?" asked Lord Christopher; "and your brother will not go, being such a young prig as to prefer this uncomfortable country in which to air his grand notions. Will you not go with me?"

Deliverance sighed and sighed again.

She glanced at her father's delicate hands, so transparent in the sunlight, and a prophetic sadness reminded her of the time when she and Ronald would be left alone in the world. Her glance travelled to her brother's rapt, almost transfigured, countenance. Although she felt no sympathy with his over-strange university views, yet the thought of leaving him alone in this country while she abided in luxury in England, smote her heart with a sense of guilt, so that she moved over to him and slipped her hand in his and rested her head against his shoulder.

"Good sir," she said, "I will remain with Ronald and with father, but with all my heart I thank you for your kindness and desire that I might be the companion of your sweetest daughter."

And none of the three knew that through a blinding mist of tears she saw vanish forever the dream of a velvet gown with immoderate slashed sleeves.

So Lord Christopher went far away, but he did not go alone. He bore with him a hunchback of Ipswich whose mother had been hanged as a witch on Gallows' Hill. Thus it sometimes happens that they who have had least to do with a brave deed do, by some happy chance, reap the richest benefit of another's nobility. And thus it was with this little Hate-Evil. He found himself no longer alone in the world. There in London he developed into a scholar, becoming a poet of much fame, one who, honoured in the court, was not less revered by the common people, that so poor and deformed a body carried so great a soul. And at last he ceased to be known by his stern New England appellation of Hate-Evil and was called by the sweeter name of Content.

Yearly from England came a gift to Deliverance from Lord Christopher's fair daughter Elizabeth, in memory of the loyal service she had rendered England in regaining the precious powder.

Within a few months, Abigail received a small package containing a string of gold beads and a rare and valuable book entitled: "The Queen's Closet Opened: having Physical and Chirurgical Receipts:

the Art of Preserving Conserving and Candying & also a Right Knowledge of Perfuming & Distilling: the Compleat Cook Expertly Prescribing the most ready wayes whether French, Italian or Spanish, for the dressing of Flesh and Fish & the ordering of Sauces & making of PASTRY."

On the fly-leaf was written a recipe for pumpkin-pie, which the great physician had himself compounded while in America, and which to this day is handed down by the descendants of Abigail Brewster. Also, he wrote a letter to the little girl who had so bravely journeyed to Boston Town to save her friend.

" For," he wrote, " fame is a fickle jade, & as often passes over as she rewards those who are brave & so while some of us serve but as instruments to further others' brave actions yet, than loyal friendship, there is no truer virtue & I speak with authority on the subject, having had sad experience."

Those who read the letter knew he referred to Sir Jonathan Jamieson, who on the day of Lord Christopher's speech disappeared from Salem. For many years he was not heard of, until at last news came that he lived in great opulence among the Cavaliers of Virginia, and had written a most convincing book upon "Ye Black Art & Ye Ready Wayes of Witches."

Y

THE END.